I0691699

WORKING MEN SERIES

BOOKS ONE TO THREE

RAMONA GRAY

EK PUBLISHING INC.

Copyright © 2018 Ramona Gray

Published by
EK Publishing Inc.

ISBN13: 978-1-988826-44-8

This book is the copyrighted property of the author and may not be
reproduced, scanned or distributed for commercial or non-commercial
purposes. Quotes used in reviews are the exception. No alteration of content
is allowed.

Your support and respect for the property of this author is appreciated.

This book is a work of fiction, and any resemblance to persons, living or
dead, or places, events or locales is purely coincidental. The characters are
productions of the author's imagination and used fictitiously.

Edited by
L. Nunn Editing

Cover Art by
The Final Wrap

THE MECHANIC

THE MECHANIC

WORKING MEN SERIES BOOK ONE

By Ramona Gray

His hands aren't the only things getting dirty.

Lily

I grew up with everything I ever wanted. Wealth and privilege, and an attitude that practically screamed, "I'm better than you." Only things went wrong, and now I have nothing. The people in this town don't give a damn that I live in a broken-down trailer and am one sandwich away from starving. They figure I got what I deserve. They're not wrong.

Now, I'm standing in front of the town's sexy-as-sin mechanic, Jack Williams, and offering to let him... do things to me with those big, dirty hands of his in exchange for car repairs. Things that the old me would be horrified by. I should be ashamed. Instead, all I can think about is how good it would feel to have Jack touch me.

Jack

I grew up on the wrong side of the tracks. Raised by a man who liked to talk to me with his fists and didn't give a damn if I lived or died. Taking care of myself is my number one priority, and I'm not interested in other people's troubles.

Especially trouble in the form of a stuck-up, former rich girl like Lily Carson. It's not my problem that her money, family and friends are gone. Only, she's standing in my repair shop offering me something I've wanted for a very long time. One touch of her soft skin, and I'm lost.

Lily belongs to me now, and I'll make damn sure she and everyone else in this town know it.

CHAPTER 1

Jack

"Are you fucking kidding me?"

I stared at the woman in front of me. Never once in my fucking life did I believe that Lily "Ice Queen" Carson would be standing in the tiny shithole of a room I called an office. The cement walls used to be white, but years of dirt and grease had turned them the colour of a roach. The smell was a hellish combination of oil, gas, and the leftover spaghetti I had heated up for lunch.

I leaned against my desk and folded my arms across my chest. Her gaze followed the motion, and I watched a muscle tick in her temple and a flush rise in her cheeks. I'm in good shape. Years of being a grease monkey and spending weekends at the local boxing gym have made my body hard. I reached down and adjusted my dick, grinning when the flush turned to a bright red stain.

The woman standing in front of me might have been a

rich, stuck-up ice queen that I didn't have a chance in hell with, but fuck did she get my motor running. She had since fucking high school.

Of course, she wasn't exactly rich anymore, was she?

I folded my arms back over my chest. "I don't do payment plans."

That red stain faded from her cheeks, leaving her looking pale and sick. I scratched at the two days' worth of stubble on my jaw.

"But, uh, Tom Wilk said that you did payment plans. He told me you didn't have a problem with it." She fidgeted with the strap of her purse.

I lowered my gaze to her tits. They were big and firm, and I wondered not for the first time what her nipples looked like. What would it look like to have my dick sliding between those lush titties? I hadn't been this close to her since I sat behind her in biology class in high school. Why would I be? She was the daughter of the richest man in town, and I was the son of the drunkest.

Or rather, we had been. My cunt of an old man had been dead for two years, and her old man had lost everything thanks to insider trading. He was currently enjoying life in some white-collar minimum security prison, and little Miss Rich Bitch was suddenly not so rich.

Her mother had left town about six months after her father went to prison. The rumour was that she'd met some new rich asshole willing to give her whatever she wanted just for a daily go at her pussy. In the two years since then, I'd often wondered why Lily didn't go with her. There was nothing in this town for her, and without her daddy's money, her popularity had disappeared faster than a dick in a whore's mouth. Her boyfriend had dumped her, her mansion on the west side of town had gone to foreclosure, and all her fancy friends had abandoned her. Now, she lived in an old trailer in the worst part of town and waitressed at a local dive bar.

Her arms folded across her tits, and I lifted my gaze to her face. She was even paler, and her big blue eyes were watering with unshed tears. I felt a twinge of guilt that I immediately tamped down. Her money problems weren't my problem. I had a business to run.

"He was fucking with you."

"I – what?" she said.

"Tom was fucking with you. I don't do payment plans." I grabbed the invoice from my desk and tapped the number on the bottom. "Your piece-of-shit car needed a lot of work to get it running. Seven hundred dollars' worth, in fact."

"Mr. Williams, I don't have seven hundred dollars. I believed that you did payment plans. Could you – I mean, would you consider doing a payment plan just this once? I could pay you fifty dollars a month with interest, of course."

"No. Pay me today, or your car stays in my shop until you bring me the seven hundred."

She chewed at her bottom lip. "Please. I need my car to get to work every day. If I'm fired, I won't have the money to pay you. But if you let me take my car and do a payment plan, you'll get your money. I swear. Please, Mr. Williams. I need this job. You know how hard it is to find work in this town."

"I think you have me confused with someone who gives a fuck about your problems."

The hell of it was, I was tempted to give her a payment plan. Fuck, I was tempted just to let her take the damn car for free. I was a bastard, always had been and always would be, but something about Lily Carson made me want to be soft with her. Made me want to hold her in my arms and tell her everything would be fine. I would take care of her. I'd make sure she -

I snorted inwardly. Fuck me. I was like a goddamn Hallmark movie now. All because of a former rich girl's tears.

Those tears were sliding down her cheeks now, her soft-looking lips trembling. She was thinner now than in high school but in less of an I'm-trying-to-look-like-a-stick-thin-model way and more of an I-don't-have-enough-to-eat way.

She wiped the tears away before taking a deep breath. A look of weary resignation mixed with a 'here we go again' expression crossed her face.

"Mr. Williams, I realize that I treated you horribly in high school and would like to apologize for it. It is not an excuse, but I was young and immature and a self-absorbed bitch. I am deeply sorry for what I said and did to you when we attended Winston High together. My behaviour and actions are inexcusable, but I truly am remorseful about my behaviour."

Her little speech had an air of robotic rehearsal to it. I cocked my head and said, "How many times have you done this little song and dance with the assholes in this town when you needed something?"

Her lips compressed into a thin line. "Many."

"It ever work?"

"Yes. Because I'm being sincere."

"Bullshit. You're saying what you think we want to hear and nothing more."

"That isn't true," she said. "I am very sorry for my past behaviour toward you. I'm hoping you can find it in your heart to forgive me and maybe just this once, let me do a payment plan with your business."

She might be broke flatter than piss on a platter now, but she still talked like she was Miss Fucking Fancy Pants. I actually admired her for it. Her expensive clothes and jewels were long gone. Her silver BMW was replaced by a Honda Accord that was being held together with spit, duct tape and a goddamn prayer, and she worked at a bar that she would never have stepped foot in, in her previous life, but she still talked like the rich little princess she used to be.

And fuck did it make my dick harder than a motherfucking rock.

Before I could lose my fucking mind and just give her the goddamn car, I shut down the weird part of me that wanted to help her. Threw it deep and locked away the key. The woman in front of me didn't give a shit about me. Besides, my interest in her was purely physical. Nothing else.

"Well," I drawled as I leaned back against my desk, "I appreciate the apology, but it won't pay my bills. Seven hundred, Ice Queen, or your car stays here."

A look of pure panic flickered across her face. It made my pulse speed up and my body tense in unexpected solidarity. I distracted myself by staring at her tits again. Fuck, I'd give my left nut to watch those big tits bouncing as I fucked her hard and rough. She'd look so fucking hot cumming all over my dick.

Of course, she had the nickname of Ice Queen for a reason. She flirted plenty with the guys in high school she'd deemed worthy, but she never let any of them into her silk panties. At least not according to the rampant gossip that ran through the high school. Her senior year, she started dating Isaac Morris and they continued to date after high school.

He had dumped her the minute her father was found guilty. I don't know what she did to piss him off, but he hadn't been shy about sharing the details of their sex life once they were over. According to that dickwad, she was frigid as a goddamn freezer. I'd overheard him telling a bunch of his asshole friends at Ren's bar about her shortcomings in the sack and how she refused to fuck him more than once a week. Two months after they broke up, everyone in town knew all about her aversion to sex and the nickname Ice Queen was born.

I forced my gaze away from her tits and back to her face. She was still standing near the door to my office, but the panic had been replaced with cold and calculating desperation. She reached out and shut the door. She didn't need to bother. It was the end of the day, and I was the only one left in the shop, but I didn't say anything as she dropped her cheap purse on my office floor.

She walked slowly toward me with that cold desperation still stamped all over her pretty face, and my dick jerked in my jeans when she placed one soft hand on my chest. Fuck, did she smell good. Like strawberries. I suppressed my groan when she traced her hand back and forth over my chest. Even through my t-shirt, I could feel the heat of her hand.

I stared at her mouth and wondered how those lips would look stretched around my fat dick. I couldn't control my filthy thoughts around the Ice Queen, no matter how hard I tried.

Not that I was trying all that fucking hard.

"Mr. Williams, perhaps we can come up with a different idea of how I can pay you for my car repairs."

The heat from her hand, her sweet scent and the closeness of her tits to my chest had me as horny as a teenager. I could barely fucking think straight. I stared at her, wondering what the hell she was talking about.

With that hard light of desperation in her eyes, she said, "What do you think?"

"What do I think about what?" I said stupidly.

She chewed on her bottom lip before deliberately dropping her gaze to my cock. It was hard and tenting the front of my jeans, and I could see the red rising from her chest up her neck.

"I'll give you my mouth," she said.

What the fuck was I missing? I wasn't a stupid man, but apparently, being this close to Lily made my brain mush.

"You'll give me your mouth," I repeated.

"Yes, I'll… I'll suck your penis in exchange for the work you did on my car."

My mouth dropped open so fucking wide you could have shoved a dick into it.

CHAPTER 2

Lily

Have you gone insane?
I ignored the screaming of my inner voice and rubbed Jack Williams' chest again. His mouth was wide open, and I could see the surprise in his dark brown eyes. I had a moment of satisfaction that I could shock him so badly, but it faded quickly, and anxiety replaced it.

If he didn't accept this as a payment for my shitty car, I was well and truly fucked. I mean, not that I knew what well and truly fucked was, but I imagined it was a lot like having a negative balance in your bank account and a car that you desperately needed, being held hostage by a hotter-than-hell mechanic.

I licked my lips seductively, at least I hoped it was seductively, and leaned a little closer to Jack. I'd done a lot of shameful things since my father had gone to prison and my mother had abandoned me, but this topped the cake.

Even as I offered to blow my mechanic for car repairs, I could hear the sound of hitting rock bottom. Hell, it practically reverberated in my ears. Jack Williams might be the hottest man I'd ever seen, and yeah, maybe giving him a blow job wouldn't be the worst experience in the world, but I was still whoring myself out.

If you don't do this, you really will have to turn to prostitution.

My usual inner voice had been replaced by someone else. Someone cold and fearless who knew just how much trouble I was in. I had a feeling that this new voice was the true me, the one who put survival above everything else and would do whatever she needed to stay alive.

You have no money and need that car to get to work. If you lose your job, you'll lose the roof over your head and the pitiful amount of food you can still afford to buy. You're lucky that Dale hired you at his bar. You suck as a waitress. It's only because half the town comes in on the regular to laugh at the former little rich girl that keeps Dale from firing you. You lose this job, you won't find another, and what will you do then? Your friends are gone, your mother couldn't give a shit about you, and you don't even have enough money to leave this shitty little town.

I dropped my hand to Jack's flat abdomen. Holy shit, I could feel his abs through his t-shirt. His low groan made my pussy go wet for him. I tried to hide my surprise and almost succeeded. I didn't get wet this easily. According to my first and only lover, Isaac, I barely got wet at all. In fact, according to Isaac, I was the worst fucking lay in the world. My oral skills weren't that better, apparently, but desperate times, right? I might be terrible in bed, but I knew when a man wanted me.

Jack Williams wanted me.

He'd wanted me in high school, and secretly, just like every other girl at school, I'd wanted him too.

He was a big guy even then. Big and quiet, with an air of danger about him that was stupidly appealing. I wasn't the only girl who was affected by it. He'd had his share of girlfriends in high school and after. While I was dating Isaac, he was having fun with a large portion of the female population in our town. Not that I could blame them. I probably would have parted my legs for him if I hadn't been so afraid of what my father would say.

My nostrils flared as I took in a breath of him. He smelled like oil and grease and good, clean sweat. It was a combination that probably shouldn't have been sexy but was. His dark hair was cut short, and standing this close to him, his height seemed even bigger than the 6'2" he was. Dark stubble covered his jaw, and I was suddenly itching to press my lips against the slight dent in his chin. Everything about him screamed 'male'.

He'd worked in his father's car shop since he was a teenager. His hands were rough, dirty, and permanently stained by oil and grease. I knew I wasn't the only woman in town who had fantasized about having those dirty, stained hands all over her body. I doubted that he could make me come, my sexual hang-ups were so deeply ingrained that even I didn't have a clue why I had them, but I still wouldn't have minded being touched by him. Maybe even letting him fuck me. Under different circumstances, of course.

Enough! It's great that you find him sexy. It'll make blowing him easier. Stop thinking about touching him and do it, you idiot. You need to be at work in half an hour.

"What do you say, Mr. Williams?" I tried to sound sexy and failed miserably. "Do we have a deal?"

He stared at me, and I palmed his dick through his jeans. He groaned again before his hand shot down and grabbed mine. He yanked it away from his dick and tightened his hold when I tried to pull my hand free.

"You think your cock-sucking skills are worth seven hundred bucks?" He asked crudely.

I blushed bright red before nodding. "Yes."

"That isn't what I heard. You're the Ice Queen for a reason, aren't you?"

My blush deepened, and shame flooded through me. I hated that nickname. Until four months ago, I hadn't even realized why the whole damn town had started calling me the Ice Queen. Finding out that Isaac had shared every dirty detail of our lovemaking had almost been enough to make me leave.

Who was I kidding? I would have left if I'd had the money.

"I'm good at it," I said lamely. "Just let me show you."

"I don't think a blow job from the Ice Queen is enough to cover the debt."

"It will be. I'm good at it, I swear." I could hear the desperation in my voice.

The small part of me that thought maybe the mechanic would refuse sexual favours in return for car repairs died when he said, "What if I want something else instead of a blow job?"

"I'm not having sex with you."

It was stupid, but I could live with the knowledge that I blew a man for car repairs, but not that I fucked him for it. Why blowing him didn't make me a full-out prostitute in my mind, I didn't know, but now was not the time to dwell on it.

Oddly enough, it didn't even bug me that he was negotiating for sexual favours. Maybe because I was the one offering them and couldn't exactly be judgmental. I'd spent most of my life judging people and now, for the last three years, I was the one being judged.

I deserved it, though. Karma was a bitch, right?

"I don't want to fuck you," Jack said.

My stupid and inappropriate feeling of hurt disappeared under a wave of shock when he said, "I want to watch you come all over my fingers."

CHAPTER 3

Jack

I t was the Ice Queen's turn to have her mouth drop open. I groaned inwardly and tried not to think about how easy it would be to shove my dick into her mouth. Her offer to blow me had me so revved up my dick was practically begging me for mercy.

Are you seriously going to accept sexual favours from this woman for her car repair bill? You run an actual business, you asshole, not a fucking brothel. What the hell has gotten into you?

I blocked out my inner voice. I'd wanted Lily Carson since tenth grade, and this was the only way I would get her. Even broke and down and out, a woman like her would never let a man like me touch her. This was my only chance.

I knew she wouldn't fuck me, but the chance to watch her come, to hear her cry my name while I touched her hot pussy and sucked on her tits, wasn't something I could just walk away from. And, fuck, it wasn't like I didn't want her mouth on my dick. I just wanted her cum on my fingers more.

"No," she said.

I scratched the stubble on my jaw again. "No? Let me get this straight – you'll suck my dick to get your car back, but you won't let me fingerfuck you?"

That red blush covered her from the neckline of her shirt to her hairline. "I – no, I can't."

"Why not?"

"Just, I can't, okay? You seriously don't want a blow job? What kind of man doesn't want -"

She squeaked in surprise when my arm wrapped around her waist, and I pulled her up against my body. "Oh, I want your mouth around my dick, Princess, and trust me, some-time in the near future it will happen. But today? Today I want to touch your pussy."

"No," she whispered.

Her tits were pressing against my chest, and even through her clothing, I could feel how hard her nipples were.

"Why not?" I repeated.

Frustration was etched across her face. "Are you being deliberately stupid? You know why they call me the Ice Queen. I can't – I mean, it isn't going to work, and then I'll have to blow you anyway to get my car back. So, just let me skip to the blow job already."

"You saying I can't make the Ice Queen come?"

"I know you can't," she huffed. "Don't take it personally, for God's sake. It's just not my – my thing."

"Coming isn't your thing?"

"Stop being so crude!" she snapped. "I'm twenty-five years old, and if I haven't climaxed with a man by now, I'm never going to. Please, can I just blow you and take my car and leave?"

Any lingering guilt I felt over participating in Lily Carson's desperate attempt to trade sexual favours for her car disappeared. Jesus, she'd never once had a man make her come? Fuck the seven hundred dollars she owed me. A woman like her needed to know how good a man could make her feel. And I was just the man to do it.

"No blow job," I said. "You let me at least try to make you come, and I'll forget about the money you owe me. Deal?"

She chewed on her bottom lip. "What if I don't have an orgasm?" She glanced at the clock on the wall. "I have to be at work by six, which only gives you twenty minutes. I can't come in twenty minutes."

I hid my smile. I'd make her come twice in twenty minutes.

"If you don't, the car is yours, debt paid."

She gave me a suspicious look. "Let me get this straight – all I have to do is let you, um, touch my, um, vagina for twenty minutes, and then I get my car back regardless of whether I orgasm or not?"

This time, I couldn't hide the smile. "Vagina? Pussy, Princess. It's called your pussy, and I'll have at least three of my fingers in it."

If her blush got any brighter, I'd be blinded by it.

"You don't have to be so crude," she whispered.

"Do we have a deal or not?" I said.

"I – why do you want to do this? It's not going to, uh, do anything for you. Why are you turning down a blow job? I promise I'm good at it."

She was lying, any idiot could see she was, but it didn't bother me. She'd never come from a man's touch before, so she had no fucking idea what she was missing. I was about to show her, and if I were real lucky, she'd be begging me for more.

"It's none of your business why I want this, Princess. You gonna let me touch you or not?"

She licked her lips, glanced at the door and pulled at her skirt. "Okay, uh, yes."

"Good. Come here." I sat on the edge of my desk and spread my legs. She eyed the bulge at my crotch before stepping between my legs.

She was short enough that we were face-to-face. I could see anxiety in her gaze, and she squeaked nervously when I slid my hands around her and gripped her ass. Fuck, it was sweet. I shook each cheek with my hands and grinned at her.

"You've got a great ass."

"Uh, thank you."

"Close your eyes."

"What?"

"Close your eyes," I repeated.

She licked her lips again and then closed her eyes. I studied her face before dropping my gaze to her tits. She was breathing heavily, and I admired the way her breasts looked against her shirt before cupping the back of her neck. I held her still and pressed my mouth against hers.

She jerked in surprise, her hands grabbing my thighs in reflex. I stifled a groan and licked at the seam of her lips. She opened them, and I curled my hand into her long, dark hair and pulled her head back before thrusting my tongue between her lips. I tasted every inch of her mouth before sucking on her tongue.

She moaned into my mouth, the sound went straight to my dick, and I sucked on her bottom lip before unbuttoning her shirt.

"Wh-what are you doing?"

"I want to see your tits, Princess."

"That – that wasn't part of the deal."

"Sure it was," I said. I had her shirt unbuttoned, and her bra pushed up around her collar bone before her tiny hands could even wrap around my wrists. By the time they did, I was already cupping her tits and brushing my thumbs against her nipples. Instead of pushing me away, she clenched her fingers around my flesh and moaned again.

I studied her mouth as I played with her nipples. Her lips were swollen and red, and already she was pressing her pussy rhythmically against my denim-covered dick. My little Ice Queen was surprisingly easy to thaw.

I bent my head and sucked her right nipple into my mouth. Her entire body vibrated, and the moan that fell from her mouth was louder this time, more intense. Her hands threaded through my hair and held me in a tight grip as I sucked and licked at her nipples. Fuck, her skin was so soft.

"Please, Jack," she moaned. The sound of my name on her lips made my balls tighten. If I weren't careful, I'd come in my own goddamn pants. She was going to town against my dick now, rubbing her pussy against it like a mad woman, and I gave her nipples a final suck before glancing at the clock on the wall. Almost thirteen minutes had passed. I no longer thought it would be all that difficult to make Lily come on my fingers, but I still needed to get moving if I was going to have her come on my face, too.

That hadn't been part of the original deal, but there was no way Lily was leaving my office without me having a taste of her sweet little pussy first.

"Time to touch your pussy, Lily." I tugged on her nipple before sliding my hand under her skirt. Her thigh was satin smooth, and I stroked her inner right one. She gasped and gave me a wide-eyed look of anxiety.

"Jack, please. I can't come. I can't -"

"Quiet." I gave her inner thigh a little slap. She closed her mouth and just stared at me as I cupped her pussy. "Your panties are soaked, Princess. You wet for me?"

The way she blushed and dropped her gaze made me want to fuck her so bad.

I tipped her chin up with my other hand as I rubbed her pussy through her soaking wet panties. "Are you wet for me?"

"Yes."

"Say it," I demanded.

"I – I'm wet for you."

"That's right, you are," I said. I slipped my fingers under the crotch of her panties, groaning when I felt her wet, slick heat on my fingertips. "Fuck, baby. You're soaking wet."

I parted her lips and slid one finger deep into her warmth. She squealed, her hands digging into my upper arms as she stood on her tiptoes and tried to stop the invasion.

"No, Princess," I said. "Be a good girl."

She stared mutely at me as I added a second finger. Jesus, she was so fucking tight. The tightest little pussy I'd ever felt. "Does that feel good, Princess?"

She nodded, but I could see the anxiety returning in her eyes. I angled my thumb upwards and brushed it against her clit, grinning in satisfaction when she squealed and her tiny pussy squeezed around my fingers.

"Like that, do you?" I said.

"Please. Do it again," she whimpered.

I brushed my thumb against her clit again. Her eyes nearly bugged out of her head, and she started to hump my fingers shamelessly. I added a third finger and watched as she struggled to adjust.

"Jack, I can't…"

"You can," I said. "I've got a big dick, Princess, and you need to learn how to take all of it."

Her pussy squeezed around my fingers in response, and I grinned at her. "You like the idea of taking my cock, don't you?"

"No," she said breathlessly. "No, I – I'm not fucking you."

"Not right now," I agreed. "Now, let's make you come, Ice Queen."

I held her tight around the waist and kissed her hard on the mouth as I fucked her with my fingers and rubbed her clit with my thumb. I used nice, even circles, strumming that little bundle of nerves until she cried out into my mouth. When her body stiffened, I tore my mouth from hers and listened to her scream my name as she came all over my fingers.

Swear to fucking God, I'd never seen a more beautiful sight than Lily Carson coming. I leaned down and kissed one diamond-hard nipple as she shook and moaned in my arms. My fingers were still firmly wedged in her pussy, and I enjoyed the feel of her squeezing around them as the last of her climax rippled through her. Fuck, I couldn't wait until she was doing that around my cock. I would take her bare, nothing between us, so that I could feel every goddamn last twitch of her sweet pussy.

She was a moaning, shivering mess against me. I rubbed her back and kissed her forehead as she leaned against me and panted. I checked the clock. Shit, eighteen minutes had passed, and I didn't have enough time to eat her out before she went to work.

My cock was protesting its confinement against my jeans, but I ignored it. I wanted to fuck Lily desperately, and I was already addicted to the sight and sound of her coming. I needed to taste her little pussy. I made a sudden decision. I'd drop by the bar tonight and, when she was on her break, show her what it was like to be eaten out by a real man instead of that douche of an ex-boyfriend.

Smiling to myself, I eased my fingers out of her sopping pussy and helped her stand straight. I couldn't resist tasting her sweet cream from my index finger. She made a low noise of surprise when I sucked on my finger and then held my hand in front of her mouth.

"Your turn."

"What? No, I can't…mmf."

I had pressed my second and third fingers into her mouth. "Lick them clean, Princess."

She licked and sucked at my fingers, and each pull of her mouth sent an arrow of need straight to my dick.

"You taste good, sweetheart," I said as I pulled my fingers out of her mouth.

She licked her lips. "Jack, I don't… I mean, I can't believe that I…"

I hopped off the desk and adjusted my dick, trying not to grimace at the pressure.

"I can touch you or, um, suck you," she offered hesitantly.

I shook my head and reached behind me on the desk to grab her paperwork and keys. When I turned around, she had her bra back on her tits and was buttoning her shirt. "Here."

She took the keys and stared blankly at them for a moment.

"Go on," I said. "You're gonna be late for work if you don't move your ass."

"Jack…"

I stood and pulled her into my arms before kissing her on the mouth. "Go to work, Lily."

"Okay, um, thank you."

"You're welcome."

She left my office, and I waited until I heard her car driving away before I sat down in my chair and rubbed my dick through my jeans. I was tempted to stroke one out, but I forced myself to stop. I wanted to come in my woman, not in my hand.

A smile crossed my face as I stared at the door. Lily Carson was mine. She might not know it yet, but after watching her come, after tasting her sweetness, she was mine. Tonight, I would fuck her and make her come over and over until she was begging me for mercy.

The Ice Queen belonged to me.

CHAPTER 4

Lily

"Jesus, Ice Queen, if you drop one more drink tonight, I swear I'll fucking fire you."

I gave Dale an apologetic look as I finished wiping up the drink I'd spilled. "Sorry, Dale. I'll be more careful."

"Damn fucking right you will. Take the trash out."

"I was just going on my break," I said.

He glared at me, but I refused to back down. I was hungry, my feet hurt, and I had a terrible headache. The music blared in the bar, and every bass thump reverberated through my skull. I wanted to sit in my car in the blessed silence for half an hour and not think about how hungry I was or the way I had whored myself out earlier to my mechanic.

Did you whore yourself out? I mean, you didn't even touch him. All you had to do was let him make you come, remember?

I rubbed my aching temples as Dale curled his lip at me.

"Fine, go on your fucking break. But you're taking the garbage out as soon as you're back, and you're on bathroom duty the rest of the night."

"I was on bathroom duty last night," I protested. "It's Judy's turn."

"Shut the fuck up, Ice Queen, or I'll fire your ass," Dale said.

I shut my mouth with a snap. I walked across the bar, ignoring the way the men stared at my tits and my ass. Our little town had three bars, and I worked at the grossest, dirtiest one. It wasn't my first choice, but I had no work experience, and most of the retail stores in this town were owned by women who hated either me or my mother.

I pulled self-consciously at the ass of my jean shorts as I walked toward the entrance. The shorts were too small even with the weight I'd lost, and half of my ass cheeks hung out the bottom of them. The black tank top I wore with the words "Dale's Bar" written across the front clung to my breasts. At first, I'd worn a bra under it, but when I saw how many tips the other girls got when they went braless, I'd swallowed my pride and ditched the bra.

Not that it helped that much, but every penny counted. Some of the men would tip me a few dollars here or there, but most of them just liked watching the former rich girl let her tits and ass hang out in a desperate attempt for tips.

Your fault. You shouldn't have been such a bitch to everyone.

No, I really shouldn't have been. I had learned my lesson, and I desperately wished I could move to a new town and start fresh. I would be sweet and kind to everyone. I'd have friends who didn't abandon me when I couldn't buy the latest fashions or take trips to Europe on the spur of the moment. I'd have a boyfriend who didn't tell the entire town how terrible I was in bed.

I cringed and jerked away when a heavy hand slapped me on the ass. The man sitting at the table laughed uproariously to his friends. "The Ice Queen's ass is cold as ice, boys."

I ignored their rude comments and kept walking. I left the bar and shivered in the cold night air as goosebumps rose on my skin. Rubbing my temples, I walked as briskly as I could in the stupidly high heels that Dale made us wear and pulled my car key from the tiny front pocket. I unlocked my car, climbed in and slammed the door shut before locking it. I was starving, but I didn't get paid until the day after tomorrow, and I had exactly zero food in my dumpy trailer. I'd made fifteen bucks in tips but needed to add it to my furnace fund. The furnace had stopped working, and my landlord wasn't enthusiastic about fixing it, no matter how many times I called and begged. I'd finally decided to fix it myself, but even having someone come out to look at it was expensive. I had no choice, though. It was dropping below freezing at night, and it didn't seem to matter how many blankets I piled on my bed, I was never really warm anymore.

I wanted to cry, but instead, I rubbed at the skin under my eyes and tried to think past the headache. I needed to find a second job.

Maybe you could do prostitution as a second job?

My usual inner voice had replaced my survival inner voice. I wished she had stayed away. She was a judgmental bitch, and I was already feeling horrified by what I had done earlier.

Leave me alone, I thought wearily.

I'm just saying. You seemed to enjoy it so much with that dirty mechanic. Why not see if you can make a little money from it? Get your furnace fixed, and maybe get some food in your belly.

I tuned out the bitchiness. I didn't want to think about having sex with men to avoid freezing to death. Besides, just because I'd finally had an orgasm with a man didn't mean it would always happen now. Jack Williams might have made me come, but there was a huge difference between letting a man stick his fingers in my pussy and fucking them for money.

I had zero sex skills, something that Isaac had reminded me of every single time we had sex, and I couldn't make money from something I sucked at.

All you have to do is lie there and spread your legs.

Survival inner voice was back, and she sounded annoyed. She had a point, but Jesus, going from the richest family in town to letting the local mechanic finger me to get out of paying a bill was a hard pill to swallow.

The knock on my window scared the hell out of me. I screeched like a banshee and grabbed at my chest. The neon lights from the bar made it easy to see who it was. I stared at him like an idiot until he said, "Unlock the door, Princess."

Moving in a daze, I unlocked my door, and Jack opened it and bent down. "What are you doing out here?"

"I'm on my break."

"Good timing," he said. "Come with me."

He took my hand and pulled me out of the car. I stumbled in my heels, and he caught me with a heavy arm around my waist. I didn't object when he palmed my ass and squeezed it. "Fuck, these shorts are too small. Everyone can see your fucking ass."

I shrugged. "Part of the uniform."

I was shivering, and he scowled. "C'mon."

"Where are we going?"

"My truck."

I followed him to his truck. My head still hurt, and when Jack opened the passenger door of his truck, we both heard my stomach growl loudly. I pressed my hand against my abdomen. "Uh, sorry."

He boosted me into the truck. "Move to the middle."

I slid over on the bench seat, and he climbed in behind me and sat on the passenger seat before slamming the door shut. I started to slide toward the driver's side, and he made a low sound of disapproval. His arm was around my waist again, and he pulled me back against him. I twitched when he cupped my breast.

"Where the fuck is your bra?"

He sounded pissed off, and I glanced at him. "I make better tips if I don't wear one."

"I don't care," he said. "Wear your fucking bra when you're in that shithole."

I pushed his hand off my breast. "What do you care if I wear a bra at work?"

"Because I don't want any of those assholes seeing your nipples," he said. This time, he stuck his hand down my top and cupped my naked breast. His big hand was warm and rough, and my back arched when he pulled on my already hard nipple. "They're for me and only me."

"Since when?" I said

He pinched my nipple. "Since now."

He pulled his hand out of my top – fuck, was that disappointment I was feeling? – and leaned down to pick up something from the truck's floor. It was a lunch bag, and he opened it and pulled out a plastic container.

"Eat."

I blinked at him. "What?"

"Eat this. It's soup."

He took the lid off, and my stomach growled again as the smell of beef drifted to me. Oh God, I couldn't even remember the last time I had meat. A spoon was placed in my hand, and I ate eagerly. It was beef barley soup, and I think I was making small moans of happiness as I ate, but I wasn't entirely sure. I was overwhelmed by how fucking good it tasted.

I ate the entire container of soup in record time. When I was done, Jack handed me an apple. I ate it just as quickly and then drank the bottle of water he gave me. By the time I was finished, my headache was already starting to fade, and the ache in my stomach was gone.

"That was so good. Thank you," I said.

"You're welcome. How long is your break?"

"I have another fifteen minutes. Are you going to eat?"

"Yes."

I looked on the floor of his truck for a second container. "I don't see your soup."

For some reason, that made him grin.

"What's so funny?"

"I'm not eating soup."

I stared blankly at him. I felt like I was missing something but didn't have a clue what it was. "You don't like soup?"

This time, he laughed, and I could feel a blush crossing my cheeks. "Why is that funny?"

"Because the only thing I'm gonna eat in this truck is your little pussy, Princess."

He cupped my head and kissed me. His tongue immediately pushed at my mouth, and I parted my lips and let him in. He groaned his approval, and I arched into his hand when he cupped my breast and squeezed it.

I tried to stop him when he tugged the front of my tank top down, freeing my tits to his hot gaze. He tucked the material under them and pushed my hands away. "Stop, Princess. I want to see the tits that belong to me."

"They don't belong to you." I glanced nervously out the

windshield. He had parked at the far end of the parking lot, but that didn't mean people couldn't just come walking by and see me with my boobs out.

"They do," he said. He cupped my breasts, lifted them and squeezed them before bending his head and sucking on my nipples. Like before, in his office, lust immediately flooded my body. Oh my God, how the hell did he know exactly what to do and how to make me feel nearly crazy with need?

His hand was already unbuttoning my jean shorts, and I tried to bat it away. "We can't do this right here."

"Yes, we can."

"No, we can't," I argued. I have to be at work in twelve minutes, and anyone could walk by and see us."

"Let them. Then they'll know who you belong to when they see me eating your pussy," he said as he pushed me onto my back on the truck seat. He held me down with one hand on my flat stomach and yanked my jean shorts and my thong down with his other hand.

I squealed and kicked and tried to grab my shorts as he pulled them down my legs. He growled and grabbed my wrists with one big hand before wedging his big body between my legs. My shorts and thong dangled from one ankle, my tank top was still shoved under my breasts, and I was trapped and completely helpless.

"Jack! You can't do this right here! There are people in the... oh my fucking God!"

Jack slid his hands under my ass and lifted me before burying his face in my pussy. His hot tongue licked my slit before he nibbled on the lips of my pussy. I stopped fighting and spread my legs as wide as I could in the cramped quarters of the truck.

He raised his head and grinned at me. "That's my good girl. You like having me lick your pussy, Princess?"

"Yes," I moaned. "Please, I want more."

He grinned and kissed the patch of curls at the top of my pussy. "Now, normally I would take my time, make you beg me to come, but since we're on a time limit, I'm just gonna suck on your clit until you're coming and screaming my name. How does that sound?"

"It sounds good," I panted. "Really good."

He laughed and buried his face back in my pussy. He gave my slit another couple of licks and explored my wet hole for a few seconds before doing what he promised. His lips wrapped around my clit, and he sucked hard, flicking it with his tongue as he sucked.

Shamefully, it took less than two minutes for me to scream his name and climax all over his face. My body shook as pleasure roared through me, making my skin tingle and my nipples stand out in hard little points. He licked my pussy lips, cleaning away my cream as he reached up and played with my tits, rolling my rock-hard nipples between his thumb and his finger.

When he sat up, I continued to sprawl on the seat of the truck, my tits and pussy out for anyone to see. He wiped his face off with the inside of his shirt and rubbed the inside of my thigh as he stared at my pussy. "Princess, your little pussy tastes so sweet. I'm gonna eat you out every fucking day."

I was in an orgasm-induced stupor, so I just stared at him as he hooked my shorts and thong around my other foot and then pulled them up my legs.

"Hips up, Princess."

I tried to raise my hips. My legs still shook, and he laughed and leaned over to kiss my flat stomach. "You come so hard, baby. You're making up for all the other times you couldn't, huh?"

"I – I guess," I whispered.

He dragged my shorts and panties up around my ass and did them up for me. "Sit up. You've got four minutes before your break is up."

I sat up, and he squeezed my breasts and licked and sucked my nipples until they were hard again. He pulled my tank top up and studied the way my nipples poked against the cotton material.

"See that, Princess? That's why you need to wear a bra to work." He pinched my nipples through the material, making them stand out even more. "I don't want anyone seeing how hard your nipples get."

"Then stop pinching them," I mumbled.

He laughed and yanked my tank top down before sucking and licking at my nipples again. It was starting to make me hot again, and I clutched at his dark head as I arched my back.

"Uh-uh," he said before pulling away and straightening my shirt again. "You need to get back to work, Princess."

"Right, work," I said. "Uh, thank you again."

"You're welcome."

As he opened the door to the truck, the cold air brought me back to my senses a little. "Wait. You didn't – I mean, I've come twice now, and you haven't…"

He gave me a dirty little grin that sent fresh wetness to my panties. "Don't you worry about that, Princess. Before the night is over, my dick will be balls-deep in that tight little pussy of yours."

CHAPTER 5

Jack

For the next four hours, I sat like a love-struck idiot in that shithole of a bar and watched Lily work. She was a terrible waitress. I lost count of how many times she nearly dropped a drink, and she had to write every damn drink order down in a little notebook. Dale and the other servers treated her like shit. The fourth time that little bitch Judy deliberately ran into her, I waited until she was scurrying past me before calling her name. She stopped immediately and leaned down until her tits were practically in my face.

"Hey, Jack," she purred. "It's good to see you, sexy. You don't usually come by the bar."

"Because it's a shithole," I said.

She laughed. "It sure is. You're in the Ice Queen's section, but she can't waitress worth shit. Why don't you let me get you a drink? What do you want?"

I crooked my finger at her, and she leaned closer before

smiling at me. She smelled like cheap perfume and desperation and had something black stuck in her yellow teeth.

"I want you to leave Lily Carson the fuck alone," I said. "I see you being nasty to her or knocking into her to deliberately try and make her spill a drink one more time, and I'll tell Dale how you're skimming off the till."

Her eyes widened, and her mouth dropped open. It had been a guess on my part that she was stealing from Dale, but apparently, it was a good fucking guess.

"You asshole," she muttered.

"That's right, I am. You going to leave Lily alone or not?"

"What the fuck do you care about the Ice Queen?"

"Her name is Lily, not Ice Queen, and it's none of your fucking business. You going to be nicer to her, or do I need to have a long chat with your fucking boss?'

"Fuck you, Jack. You've always been a dickhead, you know that?" She straightened and glared down at me.

"Yeah, I know. Play nice with your coworkers, Judy, or I'll get your ass fired. Oh, and you got shit in your teeth. You might want to floss."

She flipped me the bird, and I grinned at her like the prick I am. She stomped away toward the bar, but I noticed she gave Lily a wide berth as she passed her. I took a drink of beer and held my temper when some guy in a fucking cowboy hat and a leather vest slapped Lily's ass when she stopped at his table with a tray of drinks. She jumped like a startled deer, nearly sending the tray of drinks crashing to the floor, and the asshole cowboy said something to her that made his friends laugh like idiotic loons.

Lily flushed bright red and shook her head before setting the drinks in front of them. They paid her, and I watched as the cowboy held out a bill. Fucking cheapskate was giving her a goddamn dollar tip. My anger was rising, and I clenched my hand around my glass when the cowboy deliberately dropped the dollar as Lily reached for it.

Even from here, I could see the flash of anger cross her face. My small grin disappeared when she bent anyway to pick up the dollar from the floor. When the cowboy grabbed a handful of her ass, I was on my feet and crossing toward them.

She had already straightened and knocked his hand away by the time I got there. She took one look at my face before grabbing my arm. "Jack, don't."

"Don't what? Don't bash this fucking asshole's face in for touching what's mine?" I said in a low voice.

"He's drunk and being stupid." She held onto my arm in a death grip as I stepped closer to the table.

"I've sat here all night and watched you manhandle my woman." I leaned over and rested my big hands on the table. The cowboy gave his friends a quick look before grimacing nervously.

"I didn't know she was yours, man."

"Well, she is. If you fucking touch her again, I'll break every bone in your hand until you're screaming like the fucking little cunt you are. You got me?"

"Yeah, I got you," he said.

I wanted to roll my eyes at how quickly he was showing me his belly. Instead, I said, "Give her a proper tip."

"What?"

"Jack, it's fine." Lily tugged on my arm. "Go back to your table, and I'll -"

"Hush, Lily," I said. "This asshole has been groping you all night and giving you dollar tips. I think he needs to show his appreciation for your hard work, and I think he fucking agrees with me. Isn't that right, asshole?"

"Yeah," he said. He pulled a five from his wallet, and I shook my head.

"Try again."

He reached for a ten, and I bared my teeth at him. "Try. Again. Asshole."

He pulled a twenty from his wallet and handed it to Lily. "Uh, here you go. Thank you."

"Take it, Lily," I said when she stared at the bill.

She took the bill and shoved it into her apron. I straightened and smiled at the cowboy. "Smart move, dickhead. You going to touch my woman again?"

"No, sir," he said.

I gave him one final hard look before returning to my seat. Lily followed me and stood next to my table. I cupped her firm thigh and squeezed it.

"Jack, what are you doing?"

"Keeping those dickheads from touching you while I wait for you to get off work."

"Why are you waiting for me?"

"I think we discussed why during your break, Princess."

Her face turned red again, and I grinned wickedly at her. "Go back to work, sweetheart. I'll be here when you're done."

───────

THE MINUTE I WALKED INTO LILY'S TRAILER, I KNEW WHY she'd spent a good ten minutes after her shift arguing with me about coming here. The place was even worse on the inside. Oh, she had tried to make it homey – a brightly-coloured blanket was thrown across the back of the lumpy couch, a vase of fake flowers sat on the gouged and worn coffee table, and a picture of her with her parents beside it. It was clean enough, but the fucking thing was falling down around her ears, and it was freezing inside. I turned and studied the hole in the narrow window parallel to the door. She had patched it with a piece of wood and a shitload of duct tape, but a kid could have knocked the wood out with minimal effort.

"What the hell happened here?" I pointed at the wood-covered hole.

"Uh, that was there when I moved in. I think the previous renter forgot his key and broke the glass so he could unlock the door from the outside."

"You need to get it fixed."

"I know."

"Call your fucking landlord. This shit isn't your responsibility."

"I'll get it taken care of."

"Oh yeah? How long have you lived here now?"

She pressed her lips together, her slender body shivering in the cold.

"How long, Princess?"

"A while."

"You need to get your shit together. I know you're used to having your daddy around to clean up your messes, but he can't do much from prison."

Her face paled, and I could see her blinking back tears. I immediately felt like a piece of shit.

Hell, I *was* a piece of shit.

It'd been a real dick move to bring up her old man, but Jesus, anyone could break into her goddamn trailer and rob her or rape her. My stomach clenched, and I pulled her into my arms. She tried to pull away, and I kissed her forehead.

"Sorry, Princess."

She blinked at me in surprise. I was surprised myself. When the fuck did I start apologizing for stupid shit I said? I made it a policy not to apologize. Otherwise, I'd spend my whole goddamn day doing it.

"I'm being a dick, but it's dangerous to have that hole there. Anyone can break in."

"I know," she said.

"So then call the landlord."

"My landlord is Allie Dickerson."

"Oh shit."

"Yeah." She stood stiff in the circle of my arms. Lily had tormented Allie Dickerson in high school. She'd been from the wrong side of the tracks, and Lily and her bitch friends had made her life miserable.

"Why are you living here? Allie hates you."

"It's the only thing I can afford. Well, there were a few other places, but they refused to rent to me."

Her voice didn't break, and she didn't sound sorry for herself. More resigned. She even gave me a small smile. "It was actually really nice of Allie to rent me this place. The way I treated her in high school, she should have spit in my face and told me to eat shit and die."

"You have to grovel for it?"

She shrugged. "Yes, but I deserve it. I've spent most of my life being a terrible person."

"You weren't terrible, just…"

She laughed. "Terrible is the most fitting description. But I think I've learned my lesson. I hope I have anyway." She fell silent for a moment. "I apologized to Allie for how I treated her, and she agreed to rent me this place. But apparently, the apology didn't cover repairs to broken windows or furnaces. I call her once a week to grovel again and ask if she'll get the furnace fixed and the window replaced. She says no problem, and then I don't hear from her until I call again."

I swore under my breath. "How long have you been without heat?"

"A couple of months."

"It's just gonna get colder."

"I know. I'm sure Allie will fix it before then, and if not, I'm saving up my tips to get it fixed myself."

I let her go, and she followed me into the kitchen. "Hey, what are you doing?"

I had opened the cupboard closest to me. "You got any fucking food?"

She didn't reply, and I opened another cupboard. It was just as bare as the first. My anger grew as I opened all the cupboards. The last one had a few cans of cat food, and I gave her a look of disbelief. "Holy fuck, are you kidding me? You're eating cat food?"

"What? Of course not. I just…"

"You just what?"

There was a loud meow, and a cat wandered into the kitchen. He was an orange tabby with bright green eyes and scarred ears from fighting.

"You got a cat?"

She bent and stroked the cat's fur when he rubbed against her leg. "He was a stray. He was hungry and cold, so I let him in, and he just never left."

I rolled my eyes. "You can't afford to feed yourself, but you'll spend your money on a damn cat?"

"He's my friend," she said defensively. "I – I don't have many friends."

No, I supposed she didn't.

"Get changed, and let's go."

She blinked at me. "What?"

"Put on some warmer clothes, and let's go." I gave her an impatient look.

"Go where?"

"Back to my place."

"What? No, I can't go to your house."

"Why not? It's not much, but it's a hell of a lot better than this shithole."

She looked around the trailer. "I – I can't leave Greg."

Jealousy flooded through me. "Who the fuck is Greg?"

She glanced at the cat, and I burst out laughing. "You named him Greg?"

"He looked like a Greg to me. Anyway, I don't want to leave him alone. It's cold, and he'll be lonely without me."

I decided if I told her that I was planning on never letting her stay another night in this dump, she'd freak the fuck out. Instead, I said, "Fine. Change your clothes, grab the damn cat, and let's go."

"Jack, I really shouldn't -"

"This is not a choice, Lily. Now hurry up. It's late, I'm tired, and I'm freezing my nutsack off."

CHAPTER 6

Lily

J ack's house was nice. Cleaner than I expected for a man who lived on his own. Warm, too – thank God. I hated imposing on him but was grateful for a warm place to spend the night.

He never said it was for the night. He brought you here because he's going to fuck you, and then he'll kick you out. He wants you for one thing and one thing only.

Yeah, I knew that. It's why I insisted on driving my car to Jack's place when he tried to make me drive with him. I didn't have enough money for a cab, and I didn't relish walking home and carrying Greg in the dark and the cold. I had thrown my toothbrush in my purse, though. It was already almost two in the morning. I figured maybe if I really drew out the sex, Jack might take pity on me and let me stay until he went to work. It would be nice to sleep somewhere warm for a change.

Nice. So now you're fucking men for a warm place to sleep?

I didn't even feel ashamed. The soup Jack had brought me meant I wasn't hungry for the first time in a while. If he let me sleep over in his toasty warm house, it'd be the best night I'd had in months.

Don't forget you're getting sex tonight. I bet he's really good at fucking. He made you come twice. Twice! Did you even believe that was possible? How big do you think his dick is? Really big, right?

"You okay?"

"Yes, why?" I asked.

"You're red."

I bet I was. Just thinking about having sex with Jack was making me hot. Apparently, prostituting myself out for a warm place to sleep didn't affect my libido when it came to sex with my mechanic.

"You hungry or thirsty?"

I shook my head and watched as Greg finished eating the cat food I brought. He rubbed up against Jack's leg, and Jack leaned down and petted his blocky head. "He gonna shit all over my house or use the litter box you brought?"

"He'll use the litter box."

"Good. C'mon, time for bed."

An almost painful cramp of pleasure went through my belly. I took Jack's hand and followed him up the stairs to the bedroom. I was feeling nervous and jittery as we entered the bedroom. "So, uh, this was your dad's house?"

"Yeah. He left it to me in the will."

"I'm sorry for your loss."

He shrugged. "He was a drunk who didn't give a shit about me. After Ma died, he just gave up."

"How old were you when your mom died?"

"Seventeen. She had cancer in her liver."

There was sorrow in his eyes, and I reached up and touched his jaw. "I'm very sorry."

He didn't shake off my touch like I thought he would. "It was a long time ago."

We stood in awkward silence, and I searched for something else to say. "Your room is nice."

He snorted laughter. "Yeah, it's real nice."

"It is." I wasn't lying to him. It was big with a queen-sized bed and a primary bathroom off it. There was a dresser against the far wall and a chair in the corner of the room. Again, pretty tidy for a bachelor. With a little imagination, it could be a great room.

"You just need to do a bit of decorating. You could paint the walls blue –a good shade for a bedroom – and add some crown molding. The hardwood is in great shape, and you could add a rug under the bed for warmth and some artwork for the walls. The room has a lot of potential."

He laughed again. "You like decorating and shit like that?"

"I do," I said. "I know everyone in town thinks I didn't go to university after high school because I was just a spoiled little rich girl, but it isn't true. I just wasn't sure what I wanted to do yet. After a couple of years of trying to figure it out, my dad suggested I try interior design. I was always redecorating my room. He said I was good at it and I enjoyed it. He was right. I do enjoy it, but I just hadn't figured that out on my own yet. I decided to apply to an interior design school in New York. I got in, but then my dad... well, you know."

He nodded, and I was surprised to see the sympathy in his eyes. Most people in this town figured my family got what we deserved, and I couldn't argue. There were some sympathetic people, but I hadn't expected Jack Williams to be one of them.

"Anyway, I didn't have the money to go to the school after that, so I had to withdraw."

"You and your mom didn't have any money of your own?"

His question tore open a painful wound that I thought had finally healed. I didn't want to talk about my mother's abandonment. It would make him feel even more sorry for me, and I didn't want that from Jack for some reason. I didn't need his sympathy. I was doing just fine on my own.

Bullshit. You're barely getting by. You're one minor crisis from being homeless. You're having sex with Jack for a warm place to sleep.

I ignored my inner voice and forced myself to smile at him. "Hey, am I here to talk or to fuck?"

I cringed at how crude I was being, but hell, Jack probably didn't care. He was crude and rough and...

Surprisingly sweet.

He pulled me into his embrace and rubbed my lower back. "Tell me, Princess."

"I don't want to."

"I know. Tell me anyway."

I sighed and stared over his shoulder at a spot on the wall. "My mother has some money – quite a lot of money actually – that they couldn't take from us. I don't know why we got to keep it, but Dad called it our nest egg. I think he knew that he might get caught someday, so he made arrangements for us. We lived off of it for a while, but then she met Barry, and he was rich."

"How'd she meet him?"

"Online. They married, and she moved to San Diego to be with him."

"Why didn't you go with them?"

"Mom didn't want me around. Barry is, uh, quite a bit younger than her. She said if I were around, it would be a constant reminder to him of how much older she is than him."

"If your dad left you money, why the fuck are you living like this?"

"It's in my mom's name. She wants to keep the nest egg in case things don't work out with Barry."

He forced me to look at him. "Does she know you live like this?"

I pressed my lips together, feeling a weird shame. "She knows."

"That selfish cunt," Jack said.

"I never had a close relationship with her. She didn't want kids. She only had me because my dad wanted a kid."

"She's still your fucking mother."

"I was an adult when my father went to prison. Technically, I wasn't her responsibility anymore."

"Your old man know she did this to you?"

"No, and it's going to stay that way. He worships my mother, and it was hard enough for him when she divorced him and married Barry. He doesn't need to know about this."

"How often do you see him?" He was still cupping my face, and I couldn't look away from his dark eyes.

"I haven't seen him. He doesn't want me to visit him in prison. He doesn't want me to see him that way. Even if he did, it's not like I could afford to fly to California to see him. And I'm certainly not driving it with my shitheap of a car. I talk to him every few weeks and send him care packages."

"You send him care packages." He shook his head again. "You're fucking starving, and you send your dad care packages and feed a goddamn stray cat."

For some reason, another surge of shame went through me. "Dad has it worse than me."

"No, he doesn't," Jack said. "From what I've heard, he's in

a white-collar prison. He probably plays fucking golf every Tuesday. He has a warm place to sleep and three meals a day. Do you have that?"

I tried to pull away, but he wouldn't let me go. "My life isn't that bad."

Not that bad? You offered to blow the man standing in front of you for car repairs, remember?

"It's not that good," Jack said.

God, I hated how he was looking at me. It threw a bucket of cold water on my need for him, and I squirmed out of his grip. "I have to go."

"Why?" He took my hand and pulled me close again.

"Because I'm not here for your pity," I snapped.

"Why are you here?"

"You know why."

"Say it, Princess."

I sighed angrily. "You want the truth? I'm here because I'm hoping after you fuck me, you'll let me stay the goddamn night. It'll be nice to have a warm place to sleep where I don't have to wake up at every little sound because I'm afraid someone is breaking in to rape me."

He squeezed my hand, and I gave him a warning look. "Don't. Don't feel sorry for me or look at me like I'm a destitute loser. I'm not! Forget what I just said. I'm doing fine on my own, and I don't need your help or anyone else's in this stupid fucking town!"

I tried to yank away from him and pounded him on the back when he pulled me into his arms and hugged me tightly.

"Don't feel sorry for me," I shouted.

"I don't."

"You do, and I don't want that. Please, I want to go back home."

"I can't let you go back there, Princess. It isn't safe."

I wanted to argue but didn't have the energy to do so. I was angry and confused, and weirdly horny again.

"I don't want to talk anymore. Are we going to have sex or not?" I asked.

"We are." Jack's low voice rumbled in my ear as his big hands rubbed my back. "But not because I feel sorry for you. Just the opposite. I want to fuck you because you're strong and brave and tough as fucking nails. I want you, Lily."

I shivered all over when he said my name. He pressed his growing erection against me, and I wanted to rub against him like a cat.

"Do you want to fuck me?" he asked.

"You know I do," I whispered.

"Yeah, I do." His voice was smug.

I leaned back and scowled at him. He laughed and kissed the tip of my nose. "C'mon, Ice Queen, let's fuck."

I bit my bottom lip. I didn't know how I could have forgotten that I was bad in bed, but the nickname did a fine job of reminding me. Suddenly self-conscious, I said, "Jack, listen, I..."

Shit. How did one tell a potential new sex partner that they sucked in bed? I didn't want to tell him, but it's not like he wouldn't find out. He should have the chance to back out if he wanted.

"What's wrong?"

"I'm called the Ice Queen for a reason," I said.

"I've heard the rumours."

"They're not rumours." My face turned beet red, but I continued on lamely. "I'm...well, I'm terrible at sex. I'm, uh, too stiff and uptight. I can't come during sex."

He studied me silently, and I chewed on my bottom lip. "If you've changed your mind, I get it, but would it be okay if I crashed on your couch tonight? It's late and I'm tired."

He released the clip that held my hair up and then wound his fingers through the strands, holding me still. "Princess, you've already come on my fingers and my face. I fully intend to get this hat trick. You're going to come all over my cock tonight, I promise."

CHAPTER 7

Jack

I almost laughed at the look on Lily's face. I pushed down the urge and pulled her even closer until every inch of her body was pressed against mine. "You don't suck in bed, Lily."

"I do," she said. "Just because you made me come twice doesn't mean I'm good in bed, okay? I don't know how to move properly or… look, I want to have sex with you, but I also thought it was only fair to warn you that I'm bad at it. Now you know."

This time, I did laugh. "Yeah, now I know."

She flushed, but I wasn't sure if it was because of embarrassment or because I had slipped my hands into her jeans and was kneading her ass.

"Stop worrying about it," I said. "It's time to get you naked, Princess."

I pulled my hands out of her jeans and grabbed the hem of her t-shirt. "Arms up."

She raised her arms, and I pulled her t-shirt off before making quick work of the rest of her clothing. When she was naked, I gave her an appreciative look. "Fuck, you're gorgeous."

"Thank you," she said. I could tell she wanted to cover her tits with her arms, and I cupped both before she could.

"You've got the prettiest tits." I bent my head and sucked on her right nipple. She moaned and arched her back, and I grinned up at her. "You like that, Princess?"

"Yes."

"Good. Undress me."

She pulled my t-shirt over my head and added it to the pile of clothing. She studied my chest and stomach before giving me a shy look. "You have a great body."

"You haven't even seen the best part yet," I said.

She rolled her eyes, and I laughed and gave her a tap on the ass. "Keep going."

She unbuckled my belt – Christ, just the brush of her knuckles against my stomach made my cock twitch – and unbuttoned and unzipped my jeans. She tugged my pants and my underwear down, and I grinned again when my cock popped out, and the flush rose in her cheeks. Without speaking, she crouched before me and pulled off my jeans, socks, and underwear. I gripped my cock and rubbed it slowly. I placed my other hand on her shoulder when she tried to stand. She stared at my cock, and I stroked her soft dark hair.

"You want a taste, Princess?"

"Yes."

"You sucked a dick before?"

"A few times." She glanced up at me. "I lied in your office earlier. I'm not good at it either."

I smoothed her hair back, the anxiety in her gaze making my gut twist. "You don't have to be good at it. Just enthusiastic."

That made her smile, and I rubbed her cheekbone with my thumb. "Open up."

She opened her mouth, and I guided my cock past her lips and into her hot, wet mouth. I groaned and used every fucking last bit of my willpower not to shove my cock down her throat as deep as I could. I fed her more as she licked tentatively at the head of it. She made a muffled noise and tried to pull back, and I cupped the back of her delicate skull.

"No, Princess. You can take more. Just relax."

She clutched at my thighs but opened her mouth wider. I petted her hair again before sliding my cock in and out of her mouth. She sucked hard, her tongue licking and darting against my hot flesh and, fuck, if I wasn't already close to blowing my load in her mouth.

The way her lips stretched around my dick, the look of pure hunger on her face as she sucked so eagerly, made me hotter than fucking fire. I pulled out and groaned again when she leaned forward and licked away the precum beading out of the tip.

"You taste good." She sucked on the head again and protested when I pulled my dick out of her mouth.

"Stop." My voice was hoarse, and my thighs were shaking. "No more, Princess."

She gave me an anxious look as I lifted her to her feet. "I told you I wasn't good at it."

I barked harsh laughter as I pressed my dick against her flat stomach. "That's not it. You make me so hot, I was about to come in your mouth."

"Uh, that's fine. I don't mind if you do."

Holy fuck. My little Ice Queen was trying to kill me. I

shoved away the image of her pretty little mouth working hard at swallowing every last bit of my jizz. "Not this time, Princess. I want to be inside of you when I come."

Her alarm was written all over her face. "You can't do that. I'm not on the pill."

I leaned down and kissed her hard on the mouth. I liked that I could taste myself on her tongue and lips. I pulled my mouth from hers and stroked her cheekbone again. "I'll use a condom."

"I have one in my purse."

"I've got some here."

I wanted to take her bare. Hell, I would have taken her bare if she hadn't said anything. The urge to have nothing between us was almost too strong to resist. I had no idea if my sudden desire to knock Lily Carson up with my kid was because everyone would know she belonged to me or if my goddamn biological daddy clock was ticking. Either way, Lily was mine now, and I couldn't wait to see her grow big with my baby.

"What are you doing?" Lily asked.

I realized I was rubbing my hand back and forth over her belly as if my kid was already in there, and I snatched my hand back. "Nothing. C'mon, Princess, time for you to come on my cock."

I fucking loved the way she blushed whenever I said something crude. It made her satin skin even more irresistible. I led her to the bed and cupped her breast before kissing her again. I kissed her until she was moaning into my mouth and rubbing her perfect pussy against me. I wanted to take my time, wanted to explore every inch of her soft skin with my lips and tongue, but I needed her badly. Next time, I'd take it slow, but right now? Right now, I needed to be deep in her tight pussy before I lost my fucking mind.

"You wet enough to take my cock?" I licked her bottom lip.

"I – yes, I think so."

"Think so? Spread your legs, Princess. Let's find out." I stroked her lower belly, grinning when she parted her legs immediately.

I cupped her pussy, rubbing my palm against the short patch of dark hair at the top of it as I stroked her swollen clit with my fingers.

"Oh, oh my God," she moaned again.

"Pretty wet," I announced, "but not wet enough to take my dick. Not yet."

I pushed her onto her back on the bed and shoved her legs wide open. I studied her pink pussy, her plump little lips were wet and begging for my tongue, and her clit was peeking out from between them.

"Jack," she said uncertainly, "what are you doing?"

"Looking at my woman's pretty pussy," I said. "I've never had such a pretty one belong to me."

"It's not yours," she said.

"It is." My voice was calm and unapologetic. Before she could argue again, I settled between her legs, buried my face into her hot pussy and went to work. Immediately, her tiny hands were clutching at my head, and she was shoving her snatch into my face so hard I could barely breathe. I didn't mind. I fucking loved her reaction when I was eating her out. How the fuck that asshole ex-boyfriend ever thought she was cold was beyond me.

I licked and sucked on her sweet-tasting clit until she was about three seconds from coming. When I pulled away, wiping my soaking wet face on the sheets, her loud cry of protest nearly deafened me. I grinned at her. 'Not yet, Princess."

She let loose with a string of curses that would have made a sailor blush. I laughed and kissed her flat stomach. "You're gonna come on my cock, remember?"

"I can't," she practically wailed as I reached into my nightstand and pulled out a condom. I rolled it on as she sat up and gave me a desperate look. "Jack, please. I was so close."

"I know." I relaxed on my back. "Climb on, Princess."

She eyed my large dick with trepidation before straddling me. I cupped her perfect tits and played with her nipples until she was grinding her pussy against my hard stomach.

"Oh," she moaned as she rubbed harder. "Oh, that's so good, that's so... no, Jack! Stop it!"

I had gripped her hips and forced her to stop moving. She glared at me, and I could see she was itching to smack me. Her glare turned to a pout. "I hate you."

"No, you're gonna fucking love me as soon as I give you my dick," I said with another laugh. "Lift up."

She braced her hands on my chest and raised her lower body. I rubbed her pussy for a few seconds before guiding my dick to her hot hole. As she lowered her pussy down over my dick, we made identical moans of need. Holy fuck, she was so goddamn tight.

"It's too big," she complained. She stopped lowering herself over my dick.

"It isn't." I cupped her hips and forced her to take more.

"Oh God. It is."

"You're doing great, sweetheart. Keep going."

"Thanks for the pep talk, Coach," she snapped.

The sarcasm in her voice made me laugh, and she gasped before suddenly pushing hard. Her pussy swallowed my dick like it was made for it. She gave me a surprised look when she took the final few inches. "I took it all."

"Good girl. Now, fuck me."

She gave me a nervous look before moving her hips up and down. I groaned, and my fingers dug into her hips as she moved with slow, deliberate strokes. "Is this, I mean, does it feel okay?"

"Princess, it feels fucking amazing. Move faster."

She did what I asked and made a little squeak of surprise when I started meeting each of her thrusts. She was a little awkward at first, but it didn't take long for us to fall into rhythm. When she started to pant and moan and toss her head back and forth, I sat up, flipped her onto her back and slid my dick back home into her sweet little pussy.

"It feels so good," she moaned. "You're so thick, it feels... crazy good."

She hooked her legs around my waist, and I leaned down and sucked on her nipples until she was wiggling and squealing under me. I propped myself up on my hands and stared at her bouncing tits as I pounded into her. I wasn't sweet about it. My woman needed to know what it was like to have a proper fucking.

She clung to me, her hips rising to meet mine. Our bodies slapped against each other, and when I felt her pussy start to flutter around me, I whispered into her ear, "You gonna come for me now, Princess?"

"Yes!" she shouted. "Oh God, oh fuck, oh God, yes!"

I grinned with satisfaction when she came with a shriek that rattled the goddamn windows. I thrust harder and faster. Her pussy was squeezing around me like a vice, and I moaned her name before sliding in deep one last time and coming hard. I shook above her, throwing my head back and shouting my own hoarse cry of pleasure as her tight little pussy milked my dick with hard and rhythmic pulses.

When I finally collapsed against her, panting like I'd just run a goddamn marathon, she stroked my back with her soft hands. I kissed her damp neck and rolled off of her before disposing of the condom. I pulled the covers over both of us and relaxed on my back. She curled into me like a tired kitten. She was undoubtedly exhausted. She obviously didn't sleep well at her piece-of-shit trailer.

She yawned and rubbed her hand across my chest. "I came, and I didn't even have to touch my clit. I can't believe it."

"You're welcome."

She giggled sleepily, and I curved my arm around her, holding her against me. Her voice thick with sleep, she said, "Should I go now?"

"No. Go to sleep." I rubbed her lower back as she snuggled closer.

"Was I terrible at sex?"

"You were perfect, sweetheart. Go to sleep now."

"'Kay. Night, Jack."

"Good night."

Her breathing slowed and deepened within a few minutes. I stared at the ceiling as I rubbed circles across her back. Lily didn't realize it yet, but she wasn't going anywhere. She was mine now. Later today, I'd take her back to her trailer and help her pack up her shit. She was moving in with me so I could be sure she was safe.

I made a grunt of surprise when the damn cat jumped up on my bed. I glared at him and made a shooing motion with my free hand. He ignored me and, purring loudly, stretched out across my legs. Well, shit. Guess I had a goddamn cat now too.

CHAPTER 8

Lily

I didn't mean to sleep so long. But yesterday was a long and profoundly weird day, and my body definitely wasn't used to three orgasms in less than twenty-four hours. Feeling safe and protected in Jack's arms, I'd fallen into a rare dream-free sleep that I didn't wake from until almost noon.

"Jack?" I called again as I walked down the stairs. I was wearing just his shirt, and I tugged at the hem. I was pretty sure he wasn't here, he had a business to run after all, but I peeked into all the rooms anyway before wandering back upstairs. Why hadn't he woken me? We didn't know each other that well, and most people didn't leave virtual strangers alone in their house.

I sat on the bed and smiled at how Greg was curled up on Jack's pillow. I rubbed his head, and he purred before tucking into himself. He was enjoying the warm house.

So are you. It's warm, and you don't have to worry about

someone breaking in. Not to mention that Jack is actually a pretty good guy. Plus, he makes you come. You should stay.

I laughed out loud. Stay? I couldn't just invite myself to live at Jack's house. What the hell was wrong with me? Jack had wanted to fuck me, that much was obvious, but he had, and now we'd go back to being strangers. I wasn't good enough at sex to keep his interest, and besides, I was the laughingstock of the entire town. Oh, and completely broke and friendless.

Jack had his own business, friends, and a nice house. He would never want an actual relationship with me.

He said you belong to him.

No, he said my pussy belonged to him. Big difference. He didn't mean it anyway – he just liked the dirty talk, that was all. It got him going.

It gets you going, too.

Yeah, it did. I would add it to the list of things I had learned about myself in the last twenty-four hours.

-Will offer my mechanic a blow job for car repairs

-Will let my mechanic finger me in his office

-Will let my mechanic eat me out in his truck

-Will let my mechanic fuck me for a warm place to sleep

-Will enjoy the dirty talk from a certain mechanic with an incredible body and the ability to make me come like a fire hydrant

I couldn't deny that I enjoyed not just the dirty talk but all of it. I wanted Jack to do those things to me. In his office yesterday, I'd had my first taste of what it was like to orgasm with a man, and now I was suddenly addicted to it. If I were being honest with myself, I didn't want to live with Jack for warmth or security. I wanted to live with him for the orgasms and the chance to see if maybe we could be something more.

God, I was so fucked up. It wasn't even funny.

Depression filled me up like water in a balloon. I should have been dressing and leaving Jack's house for my shitty trailer. Instead, I removed his shirt, crawled back into his bed, and rested my head next to Greg's on the pillow. He purred and stretched, touching my face delicately with his paw before closing his eyes.

I closed my eyes. I was tired and sad, and it wouldn't hurt to sleep another few hours. Jack wouldn't be home until at least five. I would leave before he returned, but I'd use the next few hours to take advantage of his warm house and bed.

IN MY DREAM, JACK WAS CURLED UP BEHIND ME. HIS BIG HAND was cupping my breast, pulling gently on my nipple as he kissed my neck. I lifted my chin, giving him better access to my throat. His kiss turned into a suck, a bite to show others that I belonged to him. The thought of belonging to him sent a little spasm of pleasure through my belly. I ground my ass against his hard cock and reveled in the low groan he made.

This was the best dream ever.

"Open your eyes, Princess."

I tried to ignore his low voice. If I opened my eyes, the dream would end. I didn't want it to end. I wanted him to touch me and fuck me and -

"Wake up."

I grumbled and opened my eyes reluctantly. I blinked and stared at the wall in front of me. The afternoon sun shone beams of light across the floor. God, I wish I could have slept even just a little longer. It was such a nice dream.

"Do you have any idea how much I like coming home and finding you warm and naked in my bed, Princess?"

I jerked wildly, but Jack's hand on my breast kept me firmly against him.

Holy shit. Not a dream.

"Jack?" My voice was froggy with sleep, and I couldn't stop my moan when Jack flicked my nipple and licked the curve of my throat.

"Wh-what are you doing here?"

"It's my bed, Princess."

I flushed and tried to get out of bed. Jack made a noise of disapproval and pulled me even closer, his big hand squeezing my breast.

"I'm sorry. I didn't realize I had slept so long." My apology sounded super lame even to me. Jack's warm hand continued to cup my breast, and when his long fingers pinched my nipple, I squealed and arched my back into his touch.

"Jack, please, I have to go. I have to be at work by seven and -"

"It's only three, Princess." His hand caressed between my breasts before tracing circles on my ribs.

"What? Did you – why aren't you at work?"

"I took the day off. You can do that when you're the boss." His low chuckle made my stomach muscles flutter. Or maybe it was his hand rubbing just below my belly button that made them flutter.

"Oh. Okay, well, I should probably, uh, leave now."

Before I could squirm free, Jack pushed his hand between my thighs and cupped my pussy. I immediately parted my legs wide, feeling kind of sluttish but not caring, and he pressed a kiss against my neck.

"I think you need another fucking first. Don't you?"

"Yes." I ground my ass against his cock. "Yes, I need that."

He fingered my clit, sending little shockwaves of pleasure up and down my spine.

"You like that, sweetheart?"

"So much," I moaned. "You're so good at this."

"That's right, I am. I'm going to make my little Princess feel so good. I'm going to give her a nice, slow fuck."

"Condom," I gasped. "We need a condom."

He took my hand and shoved it between our bodies to where his cock was pressing against my ass. "Already taken care of, sweetheart."

I touched the thin rubber, and then he tugged my hand away before resuming the slow exploration of my pussy. I arched against his hand when he slid two fingers into me. I clenched around them, unable to hold back my moan of disappointment. They felt good, but I wanted more. I wanted his thick cock.

"You need more, sweetheart?"

It was like he was reading my damn mind. "Yes. Yes, please."

He pulled his fingers out of my wet pussy and showed them to me. "Look how wet you are for me."

I turned my head and kissed him hard on the mouth. "You do that to me."

He kissed me again, and this one was slow, thorough, and perfect. I sucked on his tongue, and he moaned into my mouth before pulling back. "Shit, sweetheart, you're so fucking hot."

"No, I'm the Ice Queen."

Why the hell did I say that? What was wrong with me?

Jack laughed and shook his head. "Trust me, you're not. That dick ex-boyfriend of yours was wrong. You're not the Ice Queen, sweetheart. You're the Fire Goddess."

I burst into laughter, a little worried that Jack would be offended but completely unable to stop myself. To my delight, Jack laughed before pressing a kiss against my mouth.

"Did you ever think I'd be such a fucking cheeseball?"

"No," I giggled, "I didn't."

"Your fault," he announced.

I gave him a mock scowl. "How is it my fault that you're a – ohhh…. oh my God."

Jack had slid his hand between my thighs again and given my clit a light pinch. It felt amazing, and I clutched at his thick forearm. "Do that again."

"What? This?" He pinched my clit again, and I squealed and dug my nails into his arm.

"Holy fuck!"

He laughed and rubbed his dick against my ass. "Language, sweetheart."

"Again," I begged.

"Not yet."

"Jack!" I smacked his arm in protest, and he nipped at my neck before lifting my leg. He shifted behind me. I felt his cock brush against my clit, and he moved again and… oh God, there it was. The head of his cock sunk into my pussy. I pushed back against him as he lifted my leg a little higher and moved down a bit more to get the right angle. He pushed, and I looked between my legs, watching in fascination as my pussy took inch after inch of his thick cock.

"Fuck, that's good," he breathed into my ear.

"Please," I moaned.

He gripped my hip with his warm hand and fucked me with slow, deep strokes that made me feel nearly delirious with pleasure. I didn't think it was possible, but this was even better than last night. The position made him go so deep, and I could feel every inch of his thick cock sliding in and out.

It wasn't long before I squeezed his arm and begged him

to move faster. He ignored me, his fingers moving from my hip to pull almost lazily at my rock-hard nipples. I pressed back against him, grinding my ass against his pelvis as I pleaded for my release. I was so close, but I needed harder thrusts. I needed him to touch my clit.

He kissed the top of my shoulder. "You're so fucking hot, Lily. I love your tits and your hot pussy. You belong to me. I'm gonna fuck you every day, eat your sweet pussy, fuck your mouth with my cock and make you swallow my cum. You're mine."

Oh God. I was about to lose my mind. His dirty talk, the way he tugged on my nipples, and the feel of his cock sliding in and out of my pussy was driving me insane with need.

I shoved my hand between my thighs, but before I could even brush my fingers across my clit, Jack grabbed my arm and tugged my hand away.

"No!" I tried to pull free, but he nipped my shoulder and thrust harder, sending fresh need through me.

"Behave, Princess."

"Please!"

His hand moved to the top of my pussy and rubbed the soft hair. "Mine. Say it, sweetheart."

"Yours!" I cried. "Please, Jack!"

"Mine," he murmured into my ear. His fingers parted the swollen lips of my pussy and grazed across my clit.

I arched, trying not to scream from that delicate touch alone. I was on the knife edge of an orgasm, and if he didn't give me what I wanted, what I needed...

Jack's fingers pinched my clit, pinched and tugged, and this time the scream burst from my throat as my climax rushed through me. I cried his name, my pussy squeezing around his hard cock as it drove in and out. As the pleasure engulfed me, Jack moaned my name and gripped my hip. His fingers dug into my flesh, but the pain was distant and unimportant as he shouted hoarsely and came deep inside of me.

We stayed locked together until his cock softened, and he pulled out of me with a low grunt. I was panting and sweaty, and my hair stuck to my face. Jack disposed of the condom before rolling me onto my back and peering down at me.

"Don't look at me right now," I panted.

"Why not?"

"Because I look awful. I'm sweating and red and -"

"Sweetheart, a woman never looks hotter than just after she comes all over your cock."

I blushed furiously, and he laughed before lying on his side and propping his head in his hand. He traced circles on my abdomen, and I grimaced when my stomach growled.

He scowled. "You eat today?"

"No."

"Why not?"

"Well, because this isn't my home. I'm not going to eat food that isn't mine."

"It's your food and your home."

I pressed my hand against his forehead. "Do you have a fever?"

He cupped my breast and circled my nipple with his thumb. "Of course not. Why?"

"Because you're delirious and talking nonsense."

"I'm not. You already forget what we talked about earlier, Princess?"

"I – we weren't talking." My confusion was obvious.

He laughed and leaned down to press a kiss against my shoulder. "You're mine. Remember? You said it yourself."

My stomach made a funny little flip. "That was just, uh, sex talk."

"Nope. You're mine. You're going to have a shower while

I make you something to eat, and then we'll drive to your shitty trailer and pack up your stuff. You're living with me from now on."

My mouth dropped open, and I stared at him in utter disbelief. "I – no, I'm not."

"Yes, you are."

"I can't move in with you."

"Why not?" He nuzzled my neck before giving my breast a soft squeeze.

"Because we hardly know each other and -"

"We've known each other since high school."

"Okay, yeah, but we don't *know* each other. Besides, I might be nearly broke now, but I'm still not going to fuck some guy just for a better place to live. I have some pride."

"You think I want you to move in with me just for the fucking?"

"I – well, yes?" His look of hurt made me feel bad and a little defensive. "Look, can you blame me for thinking that? We've done nothing but have sex every time we're alone. We've barely had a conversation."

He thought that over before nodding. "Yeah, fair enough. I can see why it comes across that way. It isn't, though. I want to help you."

"Why?"

"Jesus, Princess, do I have to spell it out for you? I like you." He scrubbed a hand across his jaw. "Fuck, I sound like a goddamn schoolboy. I like you, I want to date you, and I want you to move in with me. If you move in, we'll have plenty of time to get to know each other."

"If it doesn't work out -"

"It will."

"You can't possibly know that." I wanted to sound like I thought he was crazy, but I only sounded hopeful.

"I can, and you know what I think? I think you know it'll work. There's something between us, Lily. You can try and deny it all you want, but deep down, you know you belong to me."

I chewed at my bottom lip. "I won't give up Greg."

He rolled his eyes. "The stupid cat can stay here, too."

"I want to pay rent and -"

"No. That's not negotiable," he said when I tried to argue.

"I'm contributing to groceries," I said. "Non-negotiable."

He laughed. "Fine. One other thing – you're quitting Dale's Bar."

"I can't quit. No other place will hire me."

"I got you a new job."

I stared at him in shock. "You did what?"

"I need a receptionist out front at the shop. Been thinking of hiring someone for a while."

"You're just saying that," I said.

"I'm not. Besides, I'm not letting my woman work at a place where douchebag assholes think it's fine to grab her ass."

"Your woman," I said. "Is that what I am now?"

He touched my hair. "Yes. Is that a problem?"

I studied his handsome face with its unexpected sweetness. "No, it isn't. I'm your woman, and you're my man, Jack Williams."

A smile broke out on his face. "I'm your man, Lily Carson."

THE CARPENTER

THE CARPENTER

WORKING MEN SERIES BOOK TWO

By Ramona Gray

He's good with a hammer, and I'm about to get laid.

Madison

He says it's wrong. He says we can't be together. But I've been in love with carpenter Jacob Marken for years, and I'm tired of waiting. I don't care about the age difference. I'm doing everything in my power to make Jacob see that we belong together. I want to be with him.

And what I want, I get.

Jacob

She's a temptation I need to resist. Before my best friend died, I promised I would take care of Madison, not try to take her to my bed. When Madison asks me to build some bookshelves for her, I can't resist. Being alone with her is a very bad idea. I can't be with her. I shouldn't be with her.

But what Madison wants, Madison gets. And now that she's mine, I'm never letting her go.

CHAPTER 1

Madison

"Maddie? Hey, Maddie!"

I twitched and nearly dropped the tray of empties I was holding. My boss was giving me an impatient look. "I need you to take these drinks to table five."

"Sorry, Ren." I dropped the empties in the bin behind the bar and loaded my tray with the new drinks as Ren disappeared into the kitchen.

"Who were you staring at?" Liz, her dark pigtails sticking out from the sides of her head like tufts of fur, peered in the direction I was looking. "Holy shit. Is that the Ice Queen with Jack Williams?"

I nodded. "I heard she was living with him now."

"Since when?" Liz gave me a look that suggested I was full of bullshit.

"Since last week."

"No fucking way. Like, I get why she'd be interested in

him – Jack is so fucking hot – but why would he want to screw the Ice Queen? I heard from Denise, who heard from Sonya, who heard from Allie that the Ice Queen was screwing men for rent money. Stupid little bitch deserves exactly what she gets. She was such a cow in high school."

Liz laughed like a donkey and didn't notice the scowl I gave her. "You shouldn't gossip about other people. Besides, maybe she's changed. High school was a long time ago."

"Whatever," Liz said. "All I know is she's just as poor as the rest of us now, and she doesn't even deserve to suck on Jack's cock. Which, between you and me, I heard is the size of a baseball bat."

"Nobody has a dick that big. It's anatomically impossible. Besides, do you really want a baseball bat stuck up your vagina?"

"If it came attached to Jack Williams, I might." Liz unbuttoned another button on her shirt before grabbing her boobs and rearranging them."

"For fuck's sake, Liz. How many times have I asked you not to grab your own damn tits while you're working?" Ren said. He was back behind the bar and gave us both an irritable look.

Liz just shrugged, grabbed her tray of drinks and walked away. I smiled apologetically at Ren and headed toward table five. My boss was actually a pretty great guy. When my dad died, his life insurance had been used to cover funeral costs and his medical bills. Luckily, the house was paid for, but I still needed money for school and day-to-day necessities.

A week after the funeral, Ren approached me about working weekends and a couple of weeknights at the bar. I had accepted gratefully. My father hadn't wanted me to work while I was in school, but I had no choice.

As I dropped the drinks at table five, the door to the bar

opened, and he walked in. I immediately felt too warm, too aware of the space around my body, as he nodded to me and walked to his usual table. He sat down, the material of his shirt stretching to accommodate the width of his broad shoulders and his jeans clinging to his thick thighs. The dim bar lights glinted off the silver starting at his temples.

I loved that hint of silver against the dark. Too many times, I had dreamt about what it would be like to run my fingers through that dark hair. An embarrassing teenage fantasy that I couldn't seem to control.

I stuffed the tip table five gave me into my apron pocket and wiped my sweaty palms against my short skirt before walking toward his table.

"Hi, Jacob. How are you tonight?"

"Hi, Maddie. I'm good. You?"

"I'm good, really good. Do you want your usual?"

My voice was too high pitched, too girlish and ridiculous sounding in my ears. I couldn't help it, though. Just being near Jacob made my pulse race and my pussy wet. It didn't matter that he was fifteen years my senior. It didn't matter that he was my father's best friend. It didn't matter that he would never see me as anything more than the little girl he used to bring cherry popsicles.

I wanted Jacob. As a little girl, I had loved him. As a woman, I lusted for him, wanted to see him naked, and wanted his hard and heavy body on top of mine. I wanted him driving me into the mattress over and over again, pinning me down, whispering in my ear that I belonged to him. I wanted him to make me come all over his cock until I was screaming his name.

I realized that I was standing there staring at Jacob like an idiot. He had pasted a polite smile on his face, but it was apparent he was wondering what the hell I was doing.

"Sorry, did you want your usual?"

"Yes, please."

"Okay, I'll be right back with it."

I returned to the bar. Ren had already placed Jacob's drink on the bar. I set it on my tray and returned to Jacob. He handed me the cash, shaking his head when I tried to give him his change.

"That's too much of a tip," I said.

"It isn't."

"Well, thank you." I pushed the change into my apron pocket and tried desperately to think of some reason to stay. "So, uh, how is work going?"

He took a sip of the whiskey. "Good. Busy. Doing a job for Eleanor Rochen right now."

"Oh yeah? What are you building?"

Jacob owned his own company. He was a carpenter by trade and picked up a lot of business in our small town. Most of his evenings were spent building custom furniture that he sold out of a small warehouse type building on the edge of town.

"A new closet system. She wanted something that mimicked IKEA's closet solutions, but with more, as she puts it, class."

I laughed a little too loudly. Eleanor was one of the wealthiest people in our town. She was also Jacob's age, twice divorced, and made no secret of wanting to fuck him. I knew without a doubt that she had hired Jacob to build her a new closet just as an excuse to get him in her bedroom. Hell, for all I knew, they were already fucking like bunnies.

Jealousy stampeded through my chest, and I wondered if he could see it in my eyes. I stared at his glass of whiskey instead. "So, how much longer will you be on that job?"

"Depends on how many times Eleanor changes her mind, I suppose. Why?" Jacob took another sip of whiskey.

"I was thinking of finally getting those bookshelves built in dad's office."

Little lines appeared between his dark eyebrows. "You sure that's how you want to spend your money?"

I just shrugged. Truthfully, I couldn't afford built-in bookshelves, but much like Eleanor, I was desperate to have Jacob in my home. Although, unlike Eleanor, convincing him to join me in my bed would be impossible. Still, I was willing to eat Ramen noodles for a couple of months if it meant seeing Jacob regularly. God, I was pathetic.

He studied me closely, his light green eyes roaming over my face until I could feel the blush rising in my cheeks. Before my dad died, Jacob used to be at our house almost every weekend. When the cancer had finally ravaged dad to the point where he could no longer do simple household chores, Jacob stepped in. He had mowed the lawn, stopped by every Wednesday night to put the trash out, and did any household repairs that needed to be done.

When dad was dying in the hospice, Jacob was there with us nearly every day. He held Dad's hand, listened quietly as Dad talked about the old days, and reassured him that he would take care of me.

After Dad died, he'd kept his word, mostly. He did take care of me. He still mowed the lawn, but he did it when he was sure I wouldn't be there. In the nine months since my dad had died, Jacob had become a ghost to me. I only saw him now on Friday nights at the bar. He came in around ten, sat in my section, and drank a glass of whiskey. He was always gone by eleven.

His abrupt disappearance from my life hurt more than I could ever have imagined. I tried not to let him see that hurt or pester him like a little kid looking for attention. He didn't owe me anything. He was dad's best friend, not mine, and I wasn't his responsibility. I was a grown woman who could take care of herself. I knew that.

But I missed him. I missed his warm laugh and how little lines appeared around his eyes when he smiled. I missed everything about him, and asking him to build these book-shelves was a desperate attempt to be around him again.

Then maybe you shouldn't have thrown yourself at him the day you buried your father.

My face flamed. Just remembering that night, remem-bering the way Jacob had practically dumped me to the floor and ran out of the house, filled me with shame. It was my fault that he didn't come around anymore, and I wished desperately I could go back and change what happened that night. Revealing my crush on him had been the stupidest thing I'd ever done.

I cleared my throat. "Well, what do you think? Any chance I can hire you to build those bookshelves?"

He hesitated. "I don't think so. Sorry, Maddie. It's hectic right now, and I don't have the time with Eleanor's job."

Disappointment and hurt rushed through me, but I forced myself to smile. "Sure, I get that. Thanks anyway."

I headed back toward the bar, stopping when Jacob called my name. I turned and smiled again at him, knowing that hurt was written all over my face but unable to hide it.

"I'll do it."

"What?"

"I'll build your bookshelves for you. But it'll have to be on the weekends."

"That's fine. Weekends work well for me." I was almost giddy with excitement. If Jacob built the bookshelves on the weekend, I would be around while he did it. I was in classes during the week and worked at the bar on Friday and Saturday nights.

"I'll start tomorrow morning. Say around eight?"

I didn't finish my shift at the bar until close to two in the morning, and I was never awake before ten on the weekends, but I nodded my head like an eager little puppy. "That works just fine. I'll see you then."

I WALKED AWAY QUICKLY BEFORE HE COULD CHANGE HIS MIND. My heart was pounding too fast, and my legs trembled like a frightened deer. It was ridiculous to be so excited, but I couldn't help myself. I was going to be alone with Jacob for the first time in months, and I was already slipping into a dirty little fantasy that involved me completely naked and Jacob bending me over the desk in the office.

"God, that Jacob Marken is a silver fox, isn't he?" Liz was back, and I swallowed down my jealousy as she gave Jacob an appreciative look. "He's old, but I'd bang him like a screen door."

"He's not that old." I scowled at her.

"He's not that young. Still, if he asked me to fuck him, I wouldn't say no."

Liz leaned against the bar and admired her brightly painted fingernails. "Of course, the rumour is that Eleanor has her hooks in him. I heard she has him building her a new closet system, but he spends most of his time dick deep in her worn-out old pussy."

"Jacob isn't like that." My voice was angrier than I intended. "He's not having sex with Eleanor. He wouldn't."

"Why wouldn't he? Half the men in this town have slept with her. Why would he be any different?" Liz tapped her nails on the shiny surface of the bar.

"He just wouldn't. I know him better than you, and that's not the kind of man he is."

"Whatever, girl."

Before I could reply, I was tapped on the back. I turned around and smiled at my best friend Rachel. "What are you doing here? Don't small-town librarians have a curfew of ten o'clock?"

Rachel laughed as she slid onto the barstool and set her purse on the bar. "Hilarious, Maddie. Just because I'm the librarian doesn't mean I'm a good girl."

"That's exactly what it means," I said. "Rachel, I love you, honey, but you don't have a naughty bone in your body."

"You know that half the men in this town want to put their naughty bone in Rachel, don't you?" Liz peeked around me and winked at Rachel. "Hey, Rachel? You do realize that just because you're a librarian, you don't have to wear your hair in a bun and clothes that hide every inch of your skin. Right?"

Rachel patted self-consciously at her hair. "What's wrong with wearing your hair in a bun?"

Liz laughed and poked me. "Do you think she does it on purpose? If I were a librarian, I'd dress like a dowdy old maid too, just so the boys would fantasize about what I look like underneath the clothes."

"Dowdy old maid?" Hurt flashed across Rachel's face, and I scowled at Liz again.

"Don't be a dick, Liz."

Liz just shrugged and strolled away. I patted Rachel's arm. "Don't listen to her, honey. There's nothing wrong with the way you dress."

Rachel studied my tight t-shirt and short skirt. "Compared to you, I dress like a grandma."

"This is my work uniform. I dress like this because it gives me better tips."

"Yeah, I guess." Rachel's voice was doubtful.

"So, what are you doing here tonight?"

She shrugged. "Can't a girl visit her best friend at work?"

"Sure." I leaned closer. "But aren't you supposed to be on a date tonight with Jimmy?"

"I was," she said. "We had dinner, and then he wanted to return to my place and watch a movie on Netflix."

"Uh oh," I said.

"Yeah." Rachel dug in her purse for her Chapstick. She slicked it on her full lips. "I said no thank you, and he got…"

"He got what?"

"Kind of pissy about it, but not really." She sighed. "I don't know. He was weirdly offended that I didn't want to watch Netflix with him."

"Uh, everyone knows what that really means."

"That's what I said to him, and that's when he got offended. He said that he really meant a movie, but if I was going to make it dirty, I should just forget it."

"Make it dirty?" I could barely hold in my laughter. "He actually said that?"

"Yes. What's wrong with me, Maddie?"

"There's nothing wrong with you," I said. "Very few girls want to have sex with a guy on a first date."

"Yeah, but I'm twenty-three years old and still a vir -"

Rachel's face turned bright red. Ren had appeared out of nowhere, and she gave me a mortified look before clearing her throat. "Hi, Ren."

"Hey. What can I get you to drink?"

"Uh, I'll just take a beer. Whatever you have on tap."

He walked away, and Rachel's gaze dropped to his ass.

"Oh my God," she said in a low voice, "do you think he heard what I was saying?"

"Nah. Ren's old. He can't hear for shit anymore," I said with a grin.

"He's not that old. He's only thirty-one."

"True," I said. "I need to get back to work before Ren fires me."

"Sure." Her gaze drifted to Jacob, still nursing his whiskey and staring at the small dance floor. "Jacob looks good tonight."

"Jacob always looks good," I said. "He agreed to build the bookshelf."

Her eyes widened. Rachel knew all about my crush on Jacob, just like I knew all about her crush on Ren. "Seriously?"

"Yes. Can you believe it?"

"No, not really." She glanced again at him. "He's been avoiding you since your dad died."

I winced. "Yeah, I know."

"Can you afford these bookshelves?"

I nodded. "Yeah, of course I can."

She frowned at me. "Are you sure? There isn't much of your dad's life insurance left, and you still have another six months of school. You won't have to drop out of school just so you can have the chance to stare at Jacob's butt while he builds bookshelves, are you?"

"Don't be ridiculous," I said. "It's all good, Rach. I gotta get back to work."

CHAPTER 2

Jacob

I sat outside the house of my dead best friend and tried not to feel like a total bastard. It was impossible.

I *was* a bastard.

A pervert.

A sicko.

If Frank could see me now, he'd be disgusted. He'd punch me in the face, kick me in the kidneys, and warn me to stay the fuck away from his daughter or he'd cut off my balls and hang them on the wall.

God, I fucking missed him.

I rubbed at the scruff on my jaw. I hadn't bothered shaving this morning. I wondered if I should have. Maddie was undoubtedly used to those smooth skinned, pimple-faced kids who couldn't seem to grow a beard. Hell, they fucking waxed their chests and their legs and their goddamn sacks nowadays. If Maddie took one look at my hairy body, she'd be grossed out.

I kept myself groomed, I wasn't a fucking animal, but I had never once waxed anything on my body, and I never planned on it. If God hadn't intended for us to have hair on our balls, he wouldn't have put it there in the first place, right?

Besides, maybe Maddie would like it. Maybe it would make her feel like she was with a real man. Not those little pricks she'd dated in the past. Speaking of pricks – I reached down and adjusted mine. I was hard as a goddamn rock, just sitting in the driveway, and I was about to spend an entire fucking day with her. What the fuck was I thinking?

You weren't. You couldn't stand the look of disappointment on her face when you said you couldn't take the job. And you wanted an excuse to be near her.

My inner voice was right on both counts. It was madness to allow myself to get this close to Maddie, but I was so tired of avoiding her. So tired of seeing the hurt in her eyes when I dropped by to mow the lawn, but refused to come in and visit after.

She felt abandoned, I know she did, but I had no fucking choice. I couldn't be alone with her anymore. My lust for her was so intense I couldn't think straight when I was around her. All I could think about was being between those smooth thighs of hers. Of pinning her body down and forcing her to take my thick cock over and over until she was screaming for me to make her come.

I shook off the mental image of being in Maddie. Fuck. I was a thirty-eight-year-old man lusting after my dead best friend's twenty-three-year-old daughter.

Like I said, I was a fucking pervert.

I glanced at my watch. It was five after eight. I needed to

go in there. I needed to measure the space, plan the book-shelves, and get the materials. And I needed to do all of it with Maddie hovering around me, with her sweet vanilla scent, soft dark hair, and beautiful doe eyes.

Don't forget about her tits.

I groaned out loud. Like I could fucking forget about her incredible tits. I had dreamed about them nightly for the last nine months. Dreamed about what they looked like, how they tasted, and how it would feel to come all over them. The image of Maddie lying naked on the bed, her heavy, round tits splashed with thick ropes of my cum, almost made me come in my own goddamn jeans. The pressure against my dick was painful now, and I adjusted again. It didn't help, and for a moment, I had the wild idea of just rubbing one out in the truck before I went in.

I yanked my hand away from my crotch and stared furtively out the windshield. Neither Maddie nor her neighbours were anywhere in sight, but Christ, I needed to get control of myself.

Maybe Maddie would leave. Maybe she would go shopping or hang out with Rachel or something.

She won't. You know she won't.

No, she wouldn't. Because as much as I wanted to deny it, sweet little Maddie wanted me. If that night nine months ago hadn't clued me in, just seeing how she looked at me now would have. It's like she had completely given up on trying to hide it from me. Hell, I could practically smell her fucking desire whenever we stood too close. She wanted to be fucked by me, and I didn't know if it was some kind of daddy complex or what, but it just made it that much harder to remember that I shouldn't – *couldn't* – fuck her.

I closed my eyes and thought about Frank, how disappointed he would be in me, and how he would hate me forever just for thinking about his daughter that way. It was as effective as pouring ice-water on my balls. My erection disappeared, and I could have groaned at the relief of pressure.

Taking a deep breath, I got out of my truck, grabbed my tool belt, belted it around my waist, and headed for the front door. I knocked once, and the door opened like she had been waiting for me on the other side.

I took one look at Maddie, and my erection was back in full force like it had never left. I stared at her as lust roared in my belly, and my pulse thudded in my ears. She wore jeans so tight, they looked painted on. Despite the coldness of the weather, she wore a thin, white tank top that hugged her braless tits. I stared at her nipples poking against the thin material. Were they the same shade of pink as her lips? I was dying to find out.

Before I could do something stupid like touch them, I dragged my gaze to her face. Her cheeks were pink, and I groaned inwardly at the look in her eyes. Fuck, nine months of successfully hiding my lust from her and I had blown in it less than three seconds.

All because she wasn't wearing a fucking bra.

"Hi, Jacob." Her voice was breathless, needy.

I cleared my throat. "Hey. Can I come in?"

"Oh, right, of course." Her laugh was a little high-pitched. She stepped back, and I gritted my teeth and walked into the house.

"I'm going to do some measurements first." I walked rapidly down the hallway toward Frank's office. I hadn't been in the house since the day of the funeral. I had stuck around after everyone left, helped Maddie clean up the leftovers and sort through the dozens of casseroles that people had brought. By the time we finished, the freezer was packed to the brim. Maddie had given me her sweet smile when I told her she wouldn't have to buy food for a year.

I'd followed her into the living room and watched as she touched the old armchair her father always sat in. Her face had crumpled, she'd started to sway, and I'd picked her up and carried her to the couch. I sat her on my lap and rocked her, murmuring words of comfort into her hair that didn't really help as she sobbed brokenly. She'd cried herself to sleep, and I'd continued to hold her, stroking her back and feeling heartbroken for her.

When she'd woken up not even an hour later, she had tried to apologize. I cupped her face, stroked her satin cheek with my thumb, and told her it was fine. Before I could tell her I would be there for her whenever she needed me, her soft little mouth was on mine.

She had tasted like peppermint, and when her sweet tongue pushed its way past my lips and into my mouth, lust had flooded through me. I'd cupped the back of her head and kissed her hard, taking her mouth with rough urgency as my dick grew hard underneath her. She'd ground her ass against it and made a sweet little moan that set my blood on fire with need for her.

When she'd dipped her head and nipped at my thick throat, I'd been two seconds away from carrying her to her bedroom and fucking her. The only reason I hadn't, the only thing that stopped me, was catching a glimpse of Frank's picture on the mantel. My lust had died immediately and been replaced with shame. I'd pushed sweet Maddie off my lap and practically ran from the house. I hadn't been back since.

She'd never once tried to talk to me about that night, thank fucking Christ. I don't know what I would have said to her. Hey, Mads, I know that you grew up around me, and I'm your old man's best friend, but I really want to fuck you now.

Fuck. All it had taken was one sweet kiss for me to forget the little girl that Maddie used to be. All I could see now was the woman she had become.

The very sexy woman.

Motherfucking hell, agreeing to build the bookshelves was a mistake.

I slowed to a stop just outside of Frank's office. I was almost afraid to go in. I still missed my best friend, and the thought of being in that room, being around everything that would serve as nothing but a reminder of what I – of what Maddie – had lost, was making me feel like fucking crying.

"Jacob? What's wrong?" Maddie's voice was full of concern. I jerked away when she touched my arm.

"Nothing's wrong." I opened the door and stepped into the office.

It wasn't as bad as I thought it would be. There was plenty of stuff to remind me of Frank, but Maddie had made a few changes. His old desk was gone, replaced by a newer, sleeker model, and a slim laptop was in the place of the ancient desktop that used to sit on top of the desk. His old office chair was still there, looking even more worn next to the new modern desk. The far side of the room was bare. Boxes of books were piled on the floor in front of it.

"What happened to the old bookshelf?"

"It broke from the weight of the books about three weeks after Dad died." Maddie made a small laugh. "It happened in the middle of the night and scared the hell out of me. The loud crack and then the books hitting the floor - I thought somebody had broken in with a gun or something. I sat in my bed like a frightened kid for about an hour before I finally got the courage to leave my room."

My heart ached at the thought of Maddie alone and afraid in her own house. "You should have called me."

"I knew you wouldn't come." Her voice was soft, and there was no accusation in it, but I still winced as if she'd shouted at me.

She was wrong. I would have been there in a heartbeat if she'd called me, but there was no way she could have known that after the way I treated her.

"I'm sorry, Mads." My voice was hoarse with remorse.

"It's okay. I know why you wouldn't. Now," her voice was brisk, "I was thinking three bookshelves along the wall. What do you think? That way, I have room for all of Dad's books and some knick-knacks and pictures."

I nodded. "Sure. If you want three to fit against the wall, the bookshelves will be on the smaller side, but they'll still look good."

"Okay. Can I help you with the measurements?" She gave me an adorable smile.

"No."

"Are you sure? I can hold the other end of the tape or -"

"I work faster alone." I stepped back and looked pointedly at the door.

Disappointment crossed her face, but she nodded and walked toward the door. Christ, her firm tits bounced with every step.

"Okay, well, if you need anything, just holler. I'll be in my room. It's just right next door, so…"

Sweat broke out on my forehead. Like I needed a reminder that Maddie's bedroom was right next door. "I'm good."

"Okay, well, thanks again, Jacob."

"Yep." I walked away from her, pulling my measuring tape from my tool belt. I waited until I heard the door shut before

I rested my forehead against the wall and adjusted my throbbing dick.

Faintly, I could hear the squeak of Maddie's bed as she climbed onto it, and my dick swelled even more.

Fuck. I was in so much trouble.

"Come in."

I hesitated. Christ, I didn't want to go into Maddie's bedroom. "Maddie, it's me."

"I know. Who else would it be? Come in, for goodness sake."

"Are you – are you decent?"

"No, Jacob. I'm lying here naked on my bed in the middle of the afternoon."

The teasing in her voice made my cheeks flush, but the thought that she might actually be naked had me pushing open the door. She was sitting cross-legged in the middle of her bed, her iPad on her lap, and she was fully-clothed. Disappointment rushed through me, and I shook it off as she smiled at me.

"Hey, what's up?"

"I'm leaving to get the wood for the bookshelves."

"Okay. Do you need me to go with you to pay for it?"

"No. I'll invoice you for supplies and labour once the job is done."

"Right, of course. That was stupid of me." She smiled as she slid off the bed. "I'm about to run a couple of errands myself, so -"

"No," I said.

"No, what?" She frowned at me.

"No, you can't go with me."

She wrinkled her nose at me. "That's not what I was going to say. I was going to ask if you still had your key to the house?"

"Yeah."

"Okay, use your key to let yourself in."

"Where are you going?" It wasn't any of my business, but I still asked.

"I have some errands to run and then meeting some friends before work."

My gaze dropped to her tits. "Who?"

She shrugged as she grabbed her phone from the nightstand. "There are a few of us meeting at the bowling alley. God, how pathetic is it that the biggest form of entertainment this town has to offer is a bowling alley?"

"Will there be guys there?"

She studied me for a moment. "Yeah, why?"

"You need to change."

"What do you mean?"

"Change your clothes before you go out."

She laughed, a sound full of genuine amusement. "Who are you, the fashion police? There's nothing wrong with my outfit."

"Madison," I could hear the exasperation in my voice, "stop arguing with me and change."

"No. What's the problem with what I'm wearing?"

My temper snapped, and I was across the room, taking her by the arm before I could stop myself. I pulled her in front of the full-length mirror in her room, dropped her arm and stood behind her, glaring at her in the mirror. "This is what's wrong."

"What?" She looked her body up and down.

"Your nipples, Madison."

She studied the way they were poking against the thin fabric of her tank top. "What about them, Jacob?"

"Do you want every guy at the fucking bowling alley to be staring at them?"

She made another infuriating little shrug. "Everyone has nipples."

"I don't want them looking at yours. Put a bra on before you go out."

"Nope," she said cheerfully. "I don't feel like wearing one."

"Madison…"

"Hold on, maybe this will help." She reached up and rubbed her nipples. My cock pressed against my jeans until I swore I could feel the imprint of my zipper on it. Her little nipples grew harder, and it took all of my willpower not to shove my dick against her ass.

"Hmm, that seems to be making it worse." She gave me a cheeky smile as she rubbed circles around both nipples.

"Stop it, Madison," I warned.

"You think you can do a better job?" She traced her fingers over the tips of her nipples, and a little moan escaped her throat. "Sorry, my nipples are really sensitive."

"Madison…"

"Yes, Jacob?"

I opened my mouth to tell her to put a damn bra on immediately and, instead, said, "Pinch them."

She did what I asked, grasping her nipples between her forefingers and thumbs and giving them both a hard pinch. She gasped, and her back arched, making her ass brush against my cock. I groaned and stepped back but kept my eyes on her tits.

"Again."

She pinched them again before pulling on them. I was so fucking hard, I was close to exploding. I reached down and rubbed my cock through my jeans.

"Take your shirt off so I can see your gorgeous tits, baby." My voice was raspy with need.

She pulled her shirt over her head. My breath caught in my throat. Her breasts were as incredible as I had pictured them. She had sweet little nipples that were, in fact, the same soft pink as her lips. Her skin looked silky soft, and my palms itched with the desire to cup her tits, to feel their heavy weight and feel her nipples beaded up against my palms.

She must have had the same thought because she cupped her breasts, her thumbs rubbing her nipples and gave me a pleading look in the mirror. "Please touch me, Jacob."

"I can't, baby. But you'll be a good girl and touch yourself for me. Okay?"

"I – okay."

"Good. Unbutton your jeans."

She unbuttoned her jeans as I stared at her amazing tits. When they were unzipped, she started to wiggle them down over her hips, and I shook my head.

"No, baby, leave them on."

"Don't you want to see my pussy?" She almost whimpered.

"So bad." My hands were unbuttoning my jeans. If I didn't release some of the pressure, my dick really was going to explode. "But I can't."

"I want you to see it."

"I know, baby. But it isn't right. Slide your hand inside your panties and rub your pussy for me."

She pouted at me in the mirror but slid her hand into her panties. I watched her hand move and listened to her soft moans as I pulled my dick free and rubbed it roughly. We stared at each other in the mirror, our mutual groans growing louder as we rubbed and stroked and teased.

She pulled her hand free from her panties and showed me her soaking wet fingers before holding her hand over her shoulder. "Taste me."

I shouldn't.

I knew I shouldn't.

But sometimes the thing you *shouldn't* do was the very thing you *had* to do.

I leaned forward and sucked on her first two fingers. Her taste filled my mouth, sweet and clean and so utterly perfect. I lapped at her fingers like a damn dog, sucking the moisture from her fingers until all of her cum was gone.

"Please touch me," she pleaded again when I released her fingers.

I shook my head, my hand rubbing my dick with hard and urgent strokes. "Baby, I want to, but I can't. Touch yourself again for me."

She scowled but slid her hand back into her panties. God, I wished I could see her pretty little pussy. Did she wax it bare? Keep a patch of sweet dark curls covering it? Fuck, I wanted to know.

Her head fell back, and I stared at the smooth column of her throat. Her pulse throbbed at the base, and she was trembling wildly as she rubbed harder at her clit.

"Lie down on the bed before you fall over," I demanded.

Still keeping her hand in her pants, she moved to the bed and relaxed on her back. "Will you lie beside me?"

She was staring at my cock as she spoke, and when she licked her lips, I had to stop rubbing and squeeze the base just to stop from coming.

"Not a good idea," I rasped out. "Make yourself come while I watch, baby."

"Yes, Jacob."

Fuck! I squeezed the base harder, willing myself not to come as she rubbed her pussy. Her other hand dug into the quilt as her hips arched repeatedly. "Oh, I'm so close."

"Come for me, Mads. Show me how pretty you look when you're coming."

She made a soft cry, and her entire body shook as she did what I asked. I could see her hand moving furiously against the tight material of her jeans. Her big, beautiful tits bounced as she humped her hand with glorious intensity until she collapsed on the bed.

I stared at her tits as I slowly pumped my cock. I would come all over her tits, cover her with my thick cum and make her smear it into her skin before she joined her friends. She'd smell like me, and those asshole males sniffing around her would know she was mine.

I watched as she pulled her hand free and sat up on the edge of the bed. Her face and chest were still red from her orgasm, and her little nipples were rock-hard. God, I wanted to suck them so bad.

"Jacob, can I taste you?" She gave me a sweet smile, and my cock fucking jumped in my hand.

"Baby, no, that's not -"

"Please?" She leaned forward. "You got to taste me."

She had a point. It didn't seem fair to deny her a taste when she so sweetly gave me one. I moved closer until I was standing directly in front of her. She stared at my cock, and I swiped my thumb through the pre-cum that was dripping steadily out of the head of it. "Here, baby. Have a taste."

I held out my thumb. Mads smiled, and before I could stop her, she had ducked around my thumb and her mouth –

her wet, hot mouth – was sliding over my aching dick. I bellowed a curse, my hips thrusting forward automatically.

I should have pulled away. I should have run from her goddamn room. Instead, I wound one hard hand into her dark hair, held her tight and fucked her mouth.

"You're being a bad girl," I panted as I slid my cock deep into her mouth. She choked a little, her eyes watering, but sucked hard. I groaned and pulled out until just the head was in her mouth.

She wrapped her pink little lips tight around it and tried to suck me fucking dry as she stared up at me with her dark eyes.

"Such a bad girl," I groaned.

She let go of my cock long enough to give me a devilish grin. "No, I'm being your good girl. Say it."

Her lips slid back down my cock. I stared at the way they stretched around my width and made two hard thrusts between them. "You're my good girl, Mads."

Her eyes sparkled at me, and I petted her hair with my other hand. "Let's see how much of my cock my good girl can take."

She opened her mouth wide, swallowing as much of my cock as she could as I pushed it further and further into her mouth. To my surprise, I was almost halfway down her throat before her eyes widened, and she clutched at my hard thighs with panicky tightness. I pulled back immediately but shook my head when she tried to move away from my dick completely.

"No, Mads. Keep my cock in your mouth. You can breathe around it, baby."

She leaned into my hand, letting me pet her hair and taking a few deep breaths around my dick. Her tongue licked the underside as she caught her breath, and I gave her a satisfied smile. "That's right, baby, keep licking me. You look so pretty with my cock in your mouth."

A combination of my pre-cum and her saliva was sliding down her chin as I forced her to keep her mouth open. I wiped it away with my thumb and gave her another look of praise. "You're my good girl. Are you ready for more?"

She nodded eagerly, her lips automatically tightening around my dick. I groaned and holding her delicate skull with both hands, I fucked my sweet, beautiful girl's mouth with hard and heavy thrusts.

It took less than three minutes before my balls were tightening, and the base of my spine tingled. I should have pulled out. I should have sprayed my cum all over her beautiful tits. Instead, succumbing to my madness, I pulled my woman closer and pushed my cock deep into her mouth and down her throat. It spasmed around my cock as she struggled not to choke, and I shouted her name like a prayer as I released my cum straight down her throat.

Like the good girl she was, she continued to swallow, even when I pulled back so she could breathe.

"Good," I crooned, pumping my hips back and forth as I held her head steady. "Swallow all of my cum, Mads."

She swallowed and swallowed again. When I was finally drained dry, I pulled my cock from her mouth. Some of my cum still glistened on her swollen, red lips, and I reached down and smeared my thumb across her mouth. I rubbed the streaks of cum around her mouth until she was shiny and sticky with my seed.

She stared up at me, her eyes warm and hazy with desire. Fuck, she had never looked so beautiful to me. I would yank those fucking jeans down and suck on her pretty little nipples for a while before I buried my face in her pussy. I'd make her come a few times, and then I'd fuck her hard and deep. When I was finished, she'd know exactly who she belonged to.

She gave me a soft smile before I could push her onto her back. "You taste so good, Jacob."

Her sweet voice brought me back from the haze of lust like a dash of cold water. What the fuck did I just do?

CHAPTER 3

Madison

"Wait, so you," Rachel lowered her voice and looked around the coffee shop, "gave him a blow job and then he just took off?"

I sipped at my coffee. It was Sunday morning, and I was tired and a little grumpy. It was busy at the bar last night, and even when my shift was finally done, and I was back home in my bed, I couldn't sleep.

How could I sleep when not even twenty-four hours earlier, the man I'd been in love with for years had stood in this very room and come down my throat? Just thinking about the way he tasted, the way he sounded as he told me I was his good girl, made my pussy wet and aching. I squeezed my thighs together and took another sip of my coffee.

"Mads?" Rachel touched my hand.

I smiled at her. "Yeah, sort of."

"What do you mean sort of?"

"He told me about fifty times that he was very sorry and that we should never have done this, and it was all his fault, not mine. Then he left."

"Ugh."

"Yeah," I said. "Until he looked completely horrified, it was the greatest moment of my life."

"Is he at your house now working on the bookshelves?"

"No." I gave my best friend a miserable look. "I was up before eight and waiting for him, but he never showed up."

"Did you text him?"

"Yes. He didn't answer." I checked my phone as if I hadn't been compulsively checking it every five minutes since he'd left my house. "I messed up, Rach. I pushed him into something he didn't want to do."

Rachel shrugged. "I don't know about that. Jacob has never struck me as the type of guy to do something he doesn't want to do. Besides, he can try to deny it, but he wants you. I'm a damn virgin, and even I can see how much he wants to screw you."

"Well, it's never going to happen now. He didn't even kiss me, or touch me or want to see my…"

"See your what?" Rachel asked.

"Uh, my um… lady garden?"

Rachel giggled until she snorted. "Lady garden? Seriously?"

I gave her a tired smile. "Jacob kept saying he couldn't, that it wasn't right."

Rachel frowned. "But he was perfectly fine with you giving him a blowjob. Again, I know I have an embarrassing lack of experience, but that sounds pretty selfish of him."

"It wasn't like that. He didn't want me to give him the blowjob. I kind of tricked him into it."

Rachel muttered a curse when she reached for her muffin

and nearly knocked her coffee cup over. Coffee splashed over the rim and onto the table as she caught the cup just in time. She mopped it up with a few napkins before standing to get more. "All I know is that if I ever finally get the chance to be naked with Ren, I'll be very clear that he needs to give me oral sex before I suck his…oh!"

I could practically feel the mortification pouring off of Rachel when she bumped into the very man she'd been talking about. His face an unreadable mask, Ren steadied her with a hand on her upper arm. Rachel's face was so red that I figured she was close to spontaneously combusting as Ren dropped his hand, stepped back, and gave her a polite smile.

"I-I'm sorry." Rachel looked like she wanted to sink into the floor.

"Ms. Banks." Ren nodded to her before walking past our table. "Maddie."

"Hi, Ren."

Rachel sunk into the chair, the red fading from her face to leave two spots high on her cheekbones. "Do you think he heard me?"

I loved her, so I lied. "No, he definitely didn't hear you."

"Are you – are you sure?"

"Of course."

"You're lying to me."

I hesitated. "Yeah, he heard you."

"Oh my God. I – what am I going to do?"

"What do you mean?"

"What do you mean, what do I mean? Ren just heard me saying I wanted to suck his dick."

"No," I said, "he heard you say you would demand pussy eating from him. That's better."

"How on earth is that better?" The red was slowly creeping back up Rachel's neck.

"Ren comes off as this gruff meanie, but it's a total act. He's a sweetheart. I could see him being more into giving than taking when it comes to oral sex. He probably likes that you'd demand he stick his face in your hoo-hah and -"

"Mads!" Rachel's voice was bordering on horrified.

"What?"

"Don't be…coarse."

I just shrugged. "Why don't you just ask Ren on a date?"

"What if he says no?"

"What if he doesn't?"

She bit at her bottom lip. "You've gone crazy, Mads."

"No, I haven't. I just – listen, I've ruined things with my crush, but it isn't too late for you. I've seen the way Ren looks at your boobs and your butt when you're in the bar. He wants you."

"You never told me he did that." She snuck a glance at Ren, who was standing at the counter.

"I know, and I should have. Ask him out, Rach. I bet he says yes."

"I'm not sure I can ever look him in the eye again, to be honest. Anyway, can we get out of here? I want to leave before Ren has to walk by us again."

She gathered up her muffin and her coffee cup as I stood. "Do you mind if I bail? I'm exhausted, and I just want to go home and get some sleep."

She studied me before shaking her head. "No, of course, I don't mind. Do you want to come over later tonight for dinner?"

"I'd better not. I have classes early tomorrow."

"Okay."

I followed Rachel to the parking lot, hugging her before we climbed into our separate cars. I only lived about a ten-minute drive from the coffee shop, and my stomach was a nervous knot the whole way home. When I pulled onto my street and didn't see Jacob's truck in my driveway, the hope building in my chest died.

I parked, let myself into the house and went immediately to my bedroom. I stripped off my clothes before yanking the blinds shut and climbing into bed. It wasn't even noon yet, but I had the beginning of a headache, I was dead tired, and I felt sick to my stomach at how badly I'd screwed up with Jacob. Tears starting to leak down my cheeks, I buried my face in my pillow and tried to forget that I had lost Jacob forever.

———

I WOKE THREE HOURS LATER. I SAT UP IN BED, CLUTCHING AT the covers and cocking my head. I thought I'd heard a noise in the office next to me. There was complete silence, and I decided I must have dreamt it.

I relaxed on the bed again. I was still feeling lost and sad, but my headache was gone, and I wasn't sick to my stomach anymore. I sat up and grabbed my cell phone. There was no text or missed call from Jacob, and my heart sank even lower. I sat for a moment and then slid out of bed and walked to my dresser. In the second drawer, buried deep under my other shirts, was a plain white t-shirt. I pulled it out and pressed my nose into the soft fabric before inhaling.

That vague guilt was already trickling down my spine, but I ignored it like always. Even after all these years, the fabric still carried a hint of his scent. I carefully unfolded the shirt and slipped it over my head before admiring myself in the mirror. Jacob's shirt was much too big, but I felt sexy as hell when I wore it.

I had stolen his shirt three years ago, straight from the

laundry basket at his house. My dad and I were at his place for a barbeque. My crush was already fully-developed by then, and I could still remember the heat that went through my belly when we showed up to find a shirtless Jacob in the backyard. He was drinking a beer and about to start grilling the steaks.

He and my dad immediately started talking about the latest baseball game. I stood unnoticed, my heart beating as rapidly as a chipmunk on speed as I stared at his half-naked body. His broad chest was covered in dark hair, and so was his flat belly. He wasn't a carpet or anything, but the sight of all that dark coarse hair made my pussy soaking wet. I'd slept with a few different guys by then, but all of them looked like gangly teenagers compared to Jacob. They waxed their narrow chests, and the muscles in their arms and abdomens were from hours at the gym.

Jacob didn't have washboard abs, but he was toned with a solid mass of muscle. His hard body was the product of daily physical labour rather than gym machines. I licked my lips and followed that mouth-watering v-line that disappeared beneath the waistband of his jeans.

Neither he nor my father even noticed the way I drooled over him. Even three years ago, despite being twenty-years-old, I was still nothing but Frank's daughter to Jacob. A sweet young girl who never said no to the offer of a cherry popsicle.

I wandered away after nearly ten minutes. It was purely self-preservation. If I continued to stare at Jacob's tanned skin, at the way the muscles in his back flexed and rippled as he grilled the steaks, I would have done something inappropriate, like try to hump his stupidly thick thigh.

I'd gone to the bathroom to splash cold water on my face, and there it was, his t-shirt lying on top of a pile of other laundry in the wicker basket. I'd picked up the shirt –still warm from the sun and his body heat – and stuffed it into my oversized bag. I didn't think about it. I just acted on pure instinct.

I'd spent the rest of the visit with a combination of lust and guilt coursing through me. By the time we returned home, the lust was far greater than the guilt. I immediately went to bed, stripped off my clothes, and put on Jacob's t-shirt. His scent had surrounded me, and I'd masturbated furiously to the image of his naked chest.

I'd worn his shirt many times in the three years since then. At first, it was only when I was feeling particularly horny for him, but as time went on, I started wearing it when I was lonely or upset about something. I'd worn it every night for a month straight after dad died. It felt like the only thing that comforted me at the time, but I regretted it now. My scent had overtaken his, and now there was only the faintest reminder of him.

I rubbed my hand over his shirt one last time and headed downstairs to the kitchen. Maybe I could visit Jacob at his place and sneak another shirt from the laundry.

Seriously? You're twenty-three years old. Can you try to act like an adult? Besides, after what happened yesterday, Jacob will never speak to you again, let alone invite you to his house for a visit. What happened between you yesterday is the best you'll ever get with him. Just be happy you got that.

I opened the fridge and grabbed the carton of apple juice. I was still upset about how horrified Jacob had looked after he came in my mouth, but there a part of me that couldn't let go of my delight at finally having proof of his attraction to me.

What happened nine months ago wasn't a one-time thing, a moment brought on by grief and despair and a mutual need for comfort. Jacob wanted me. Hearing him call me 'baby' in that deep voice of his and seeing the lust in his eyes when he'd stared at my breasts still made me wet and achy over twenty-four hours later. Tasting him, having his cock in my mouth while he told me I was his good girl, was enough material for my masturbation fantasies to last me a damn decade.

I slid my free hand between my thighs. I wasn't wearing panties, and my pussy was so wet I would ruin the damn couch if I sat down. I'd have to go back upstairs and put some underwear on.

His dick was incredible, yeah? Big and thick and so fucking tasty. Could you imagine how it would feel in your pussy?

I moved to the sink and washed my hands before unscrewing the cap from the apple juice carton and raising it to my mouth. Yeah, I could definitely imagine how it would feel. None of my previous boyfriends had dicks the size of Jacob's, but I was more than willing to try to take his massive –

"Is that my shirt?"

I screamed in surprise at the deep voice coming from behind me. The apple juice I was swallowing made an abrupt break for my lungs, and I immediately coughed and choked. I leaned over the sink, gagging and coughing up the juice from what felt like the bottom of my lungs.

Jacob patted and then rubbed my back with his left hand as he used his right hand to pull my dark hair out of my face. I coughed and coughed again, trying to catch my breath.

"You're all right. Take a breath, baby."

I whooped in a big gulp of air into my burning lungs. My eyes were watering, and I swiped at them before straightening a little. I buried my face in the crook of my elbow and coughed again.

"You okay?"

I lifted my head and stared up into Jacob's handsome face. I don't think he even realized the way he was cupping the back of my neck under my hair or the way our bodies were so close, the tips of my breasts were brushing against him.

"You scared me." I gave him an accusing look. My heart was hammering away in my chest, and my lungs were still burning a little.

"I'm sorry, baby."

"What are you doing here?" I leaned against him. I couldn't help it. He was big and warm, and how his fingers kneaded my neck felt terrific.

He immediately stiffened, and I tried not to look as hurt as I felt when he dropped his hand and put a few feet of space between us.

"What are you doing here?" I repeated. I placed the cap back on the apple juice and moved past him to put the juice in the fridge. When I turned around, he was staring at my bare legs, and the need on his face was so strong it made my nipples harden in response.

"Jacob?" I prompted.

"What?"

Oh God, the hoarseness of his voice made me weak.

"Why are you here?"

He visibly tore his gaze away from my legs and stared at the table instead. "I'm working on the bookshelves. I've been here for an hour or so. I let myself in when you didn't answer the door."

"I didn't hear you knocking."

"Not surprised. You were sleeping pretty soundly."

"You came into my bedroom while I was sleeping?"

He gave me a guilty look. "I just poked my head in to

make sure you were okay. I didn't, uh, touch you or anything."

Shit, I hadn't meant to make him sound like a pervert. "I know. I wouldn't have minded if you had."

His face flushed, his gaze dipped to my tits, and his big hands clenched into fists as another look of deep longing crossed his face. A rush of adrenaline and lust went through me.

Jacob was still tempted, and, God help me, I would do everything I could to make him give in to that temptation.

I gave him a lazy smile and crossed my arms under my tits, pulling the material of Jacob's shirt taut across them. "I stole it."

"I – what?" He couldn't stop staring at my breasts.

"Your shirt. I stole it three years ago."

He blinked and finally raised his gaze to my face. "You stole my shirt?"

"Yes, from the laundry basket in the bathroom."

"Why?" His look of genuine confusion almost made me giggle.

Instead, I gave him another slow and seductive smile. "It smelled like you. I took it home, put it on and then mastur-bated while I thought about you fucking me."

I dropped my gaze to his crotch. His erection was evident, and he half-turned away from me. "Stop it, Madison."

"Stop what? Stop stealing your clothes? Stop wearing them? Stop touching my pussy while I imagine you fucking me?"

"All of the above." His voice was unsteady and dripping with obvious desire.

"You don't get to tell me what to do. You're not my father."

"I'm old enough to be your father," he retorted.

"Barely. My father was fifty-two," I replied. "Honestly, it was kind of weird that you and my dad were such good friends considering your age difference."

"Not that weird."

"A little weird."

He blew his breath out in an exasperated rush. "Just stop stealing my clothes and…"

"And what?" I leaned against the counter and crossed my legs.

"You know what."

"Rubbing my pussy while I think about you fucking me?"

"Madison, I asked you to stop." His look was half warning, half want.

"What if I don't? What are you going to do about it?" I rubbed my flat stomach, loving the way his gaze immediately followed the motion of my hand.

"Why are you doing this to me?" His voice was low.

I should have felt bad.

I didn't.

"Because I want you, and you want me," I said.

"It's wrong."

"It isn't. It's so right, honey. Can't you see that? Can't you feel that?"

He didn't reply, and my hands dropped to my shirt hem. "Yesterday, you didn't want to see my pussy. Do you want to see it today?"

"Yes."

I didn't wait for him to change his mind. I lifted the hem of his shirt to just above my pussy. He groaned and took a step toward me.

"Do you think my pussy is pretty, Jacob?"

"Yes."

I raised my shirt a little higher as Jacob stared hungrily at my pussy. He was on the edge of his control, and I traced my fingers over the small patch of dark curls at the top of my pussy.

"Fuck." His voice couldn't hide his need.

"Would you like to see my ass, Jacob?" I didn't wait for him to respond. I turned, bunching his shirt around my waist. The cool air washed over my naked ass, and I wiggled it at him, grinning when he made a low groan.

I stared out the window above the sink, my haze of lust so thick I could barely breathe and spread my legs just enough for him to see the wet, plump lips of my pussy. "Do you see how wet I am for you, Jacob? Do you see – oh!"

Jacob's hard hands were on my hips, his fingers digging into my flesh as he hauled me to my tiptoes. His leg pushed my legs wide, and I had no idea when or how he got his damn pants undone so quickly, but there was no mistaking the smooth, blunt head of his cock that was pushing against my entrance. An image of his massive cock flickered through me, and there was the tiniest trickle of anxiety.

"Jacob, maybe we shouldn't -"

"No." His hot breath washed over my cheek. "No more teasing. Take my cock like my good girl."

Without waiting for my reply, he thrust into me. He was big, big enough that my little pussy tried to resist the sudden invasion. He made a low moan and pushed again, sinking himself balls-deep into my hot core.

I cried out, my hands gripping the edge of the counter as Jacob bent me over the counter. I stared into the sink, my body shaking with every driving thrust of Jacob's cock. My pussy squeezed around him as he angled me a bit higher and pounded in and out of me. The edge of the counter was digging into my stomach, and my face was almost touching the bottom of the sink, but with every stroke, the head of Jacob's cock rubbed against my g-spot. I'd never once had a man find my g-spot so fucking easily, and I screamed my pleasure as Jacob increased his pace. He was fucking me so hard that my feet were nearly lifted off the ground with every hard stroke. I screwed my eyes shut and screamed again as my orgasm hit me in a sweet rush that made lights explode beneath my eyelids.

Jacob bellowed my name, his large body driving mine up against the counter. He pinned me against it, one hand gripping my hip and the other wrapped in my hair as he came deep inside of me. He shook wildly as his cum filled my pussy.

He rested his forehead against my back, breathing heavily and his hand rubbing my hip as he softened inside of me. When he straightened and pulled out, I could already feel his cum starting to drip from my pussy and down my inner thigh.

He turned me around. My smile died on my lips at the look on his face. "Jacob? Are you okay?"

"Go and put some other clothes on." He turned away and zipped up.

"Are you leaving me again?"

"No." He didn't turn around. "But we need to talk, and I can't – I need you to get dressed. Please, baby. Just do what I'm asking."

"Okay." I walked unsteadily from the kitchen, confident he'd be gone when I returned.

CHAPTER 4

Jacob

She returned to the kitchen less than ten minutes later. I had poured her a glass of water and myself a glass of scotch from the liquor cabinet. She immediately picked up the scotch and drained it before plopping down in one of the kitchen chairs.

She was wearing yoga pants and a t-shirt, and while I was grateful she was no longer wearing just my shirt, would it have killed her to put a fucking bra on? I tried not to stare at her tits as I poured another scotch and pulled the glass closer to me before she could take it.

"The water is for you."

She didn't reply, just stared silently at me. I could see the relief in them, but before I could ask about it, she said, "I thought you would be gone again."

"I said I wouldn't leave."

"I know, but…"

"But what?"

"Nothing."

"Tell me, Mads."

She traced her finger along the top of the table and shook her head. Her nipples were still hard and pressing against the thin fabric of her shirt, reminding me that I still hadn't touched them, licked them, sucked on them.

Christ. I was getting hard again. I was like a fucking teenager around Maddie. I tried to discreetly adjust myself before drinking the scotch in my glass in two swallows.

Maddie reached for the bottle. "Do you want more?"

"No."

"You sure?"

"Yes."

She unscrewed the cap and took another slug of scotch straight from the bottle. She coughed and gasped as her cheeks turned red.

"Mads, stop."

I reached across the table and plucked the bottle from her hand before she could take another drink. She scowled at me and crossed her arms under her tits. I tried not to stare at them like a fucking pervert and failed miserably.

"I'm negative," I said abruptly as I set the scotch bottle in front of me.

"What?" She gave me a confused look.

Christ. Shame swept through me. I hadn't meant to come in Mads. Hell, I hadn't meant to fuck her at all. But I had fucked her, and I had come in her, and now I needed to reassure her that not only was I infection free, but that I would take responsibility for any consequences of my actions.

"My tests are all negative," I repeated. "I'll show you my records online. I'm sorry, Mads. I didn't mean to come in you." Fuck, just saying the words made me sound like a creep.

"I liked it," she said. "I would have been mad at you if you hadn't come in me when you fucked me."

"I shouldn't have fucked you." My voice was too loud. "But I did, and now I -"

"Do you regret it?"

I shook my head. I should have lied and told her it was a huge mistake, but I couldn't. "No."

Her entire body lost its tension, and she gave me her gorgeous smile. She reached for my hand, that smile faltering when I pulled back.

"I don't regret it, baby, but we can't do it again."

She didn't say anything, and I made my voice stern. "I mean it, Madison. No more teasing me when I'm trying to work by not wearing a bra or by showing me your pussy."

"You wanted to see it."

I rubbed my forehead. Madison had a point, and she didn't seem traumatized by what just happened, but I couldn't stop thinking about the anxiety in her voice right before I fucked her. She had tried to ask me to stop, but I had completely ignored her. No, worse, I had told her she had to fuck me.

Shame swirled in my guts, and now it was my turn to take a swig straight from the bottle.

"Jacob? What's wrong?"

"What's wrong? You were about to ask me to stop, and I fucked you anyway, Mads."

"I wasn't going to ask you to stop."

"You were," I insisted. "You were telling me we shouldn't fuck, and I ignored you."

My erection had disappeared, but she shifted in her chair,

and just the gentle sway of her tits made my cock twitch. I was a fucking monster.

"I wasn't suggesting we shouldn't have sex. I was trying to suggest that maybe we shouldn't have sex right here in the kitchen. And that's only because you're big, and I was afraid it might hurt. I thought it might be better if I was on top and could control the pace."

"Did it hurt?" I asked.

"A little."

"Fuck." Her admission sent fresh guilt knifing through me. "I'm sorry. I'm so sorry."

She brushed off my apology. "Only at first, and it's just because I've never been with anyone as big as you. I'll adjust to your size."

Christ, I hated how excited it made me to hear her talk like we'd be fucking again.

We couldn't.

"Mads, we can't do this again."

"Yes, we can."

"No, we can't."

She just laughed. "Do you think you can resist me, Jacob? Now that you know how tight my pussy is? How wet it is for you?"

"What if you're pregnant?"

"What if I am?"

I reached across and took her hand. Squeezed it. "I'll do right by you, Mads. I promise. If you're carrying my baby, I'll take care of the both of you."

"Thank you. That means a lot. But I'm on the pill, so…"

"Oh. Okay, well, uh, that's good."

Fuck, was that disappointment I was feeling? I wanted to deny it, but I couldn't. If Madison was pregnant with my baby, it was the perfect excuse to be with her.

"You look disappointed."

I cleared my throat. "I'm not."

"You like the idea of me being knocked up with your baby."

"No, I don't."

"You do." She gave me a saucy grin that had me itching to kiss her, to strip her naked, and to fuck her. Instead, I stood up.

"We aren't doing this again, Madison. Do you understand? I'm here to work on the bookshelves, nothing more."

"Sure, okay."

I scowled at her tone. "I'm serious. What happened between us can't happen again. If the people in this town knew that I had…"

She made a face at me. "I don't give a flying fuck what anyone in this town thinks, Jacob, and you shouldn't either. It's none of their business if we're together or not."

"I don't care what they say about me. I don't want them talking shit about you, though. You're young and beautiful and have your entire life ahead of you. I won't let you waste it on an old man like me."

"You're not an old man."

I grimaced and shook my head. "I'm going to work on the bookshelves. Do me a favour and – and stay away from me."

I expected to see hurt on her face. Instead, she smiled at me. "Whatever you say, Jacob."

She was up to something, but seeing as I was about two seconds away from ripping off her clothes and fucking her in the kitchen again, I couldn't stick around to find out what it was. Muttering a curse under my breath, I stalked out of the room.

CHAPTER 5

Madison

"This isn't a good idea, Maddie."

"Sure it is. Pass me that lipstick. The one in the pink tube."

Rachel passed me the lipstick. "It's your first Friday off in months, and you'll spend it drinking at Ren's Bar."

"No, I'll spend it flirting with every guy I see to make Jacob jealous," I corrected. "He doesn't know I have a night off, so he'll show up at the bar tonight like every Friday night. He'll see me dancing and flirting, and it'll drive him crazy."

"What if he just leaves?"

"He probably will. Jacob is stubborn. But it's been a week since he's seen me, and I know how much he wants me. He might leave the bar tonight, but he'll think about me all night, think about what he's missing. Then, tomorrow, when he comes by to work on the bookshelves, I'll accidentally be walking out of the shower. Completely naked. He won't be able to resist me."

Rachel laughed, and I grinned at her before carefully applying the lipstick.

"This plan is so insane, it might work. You know that?"

"Of course, it'll work," I said. "Jacob wants me as much as I want him. He's just worried about what the assholes in this town will say. But I don't care, Rach. I want him. I love him. And if making him jealous is the first step to getting him to admit that he loves me too, then so be it."

"You think Jacob loves you?"

I wrinkled my nose at her. "Why wouldn't he? I'm awesome."

She laughed again. "I know. I just meant that there's a difference between lust and love, but it isn't always clear."

I set the lipstick down and stared at Rachel in the mirror. "I know. And hell, maybe he doesn't love me. Maybe he just really wants to fuck me. I hope not, but you're right that it might just be that. There's only one way to find out."

I stood and turned around to stare critically at Rachel. "Now, what do we do about this?"

"About what?" Rachel gave her outfit a self-conscious look.

"You're not going to make Ren insane with need wearing tights, an ankle-length skirt, and a shirt buttoned up to your neck, sweetie."

She tugged at her skirt. "I'm too fat to wear short skirts."

I scowled at her. "You're not fat, and if you say that again, I'll punch you in the tit."

She covered her breasts with her arms and scowled at me. "I'm not wearing a short skirt to the bar, Mads. Not with my fa – chunky thighs."

"Fine." I tugged her arms away and unbuttoned her shirt.

"At least unbutton your shirt a little. God gave you the best-looking tits in town. You need to at least – hello, what's this?"

Before Rachel could stop me, I had unbuttoned the rest of her shirt and was staring at her bra. It was fire-engine red with a lace edging and a demi-cup. It barely covered her nipples and pushed her breasts into high mounds on her chest.

"Holy shit, Rachel. I'm completely straight, and even I'm a little turned on by your tits right now."

"Shut up, Mads!" She blushed furiously and yanked her shirt closed.

"That's a gorgeous bra. Where'd you get it?"

"I ordered it online."

"It's sexy as hell. You're like the total cliché of the librarian. You know that, right? All prim and proper on the outside and total slut under your clothes."

"I like pretty underwear, okay? It doesn't make me a slut."

I grinned at her. "Nah, it doesn't. But, if Ren could see what was under your shirt, he'd pop your cherry for you, no questions asked. In fact, come here."

"What?" She was reaching for the buttons on her shirt, and I brushed her hands away.

"Take off your shirt." I started digging through the top drawer of my dresser.

"Why?"

"Just do it. Put this on."

She slipped out of her shirt and took the shirt I gave her. She started to button it before shaking her head. "I can't wear this. It's too small. I'm like four sizes larger than you."

"It's perfect," I said.

"I can't even get it buttoned over my boobs!"

She was tugging futilely at the edges of the shirt. She'd

managed to do up the button across her tits, but it was straining to do its job.

"That's the point."

Rachel gave me a look of horror. "Are you kidding me? I can't go to the bar like this. My tits are nearly falling out of my shirt."

I studied the deep v of her cleavage and her pale, milky skin. "Just don't run or jump up and down, and you'll be fine."

"The shirt is too tight. It shows off my gut."

"It shows off your gorgeous curves. Besides, with those boobs, no one will be looking at your stomach. I guarantee it. Are you wearing your hair in the bun, or should we see what it looks like down?"

"No," Rachel said. "I didn't wash my hair this morning, so I can't wear it down."

"Really?" I studied her hair. "Jesus, it looks good. I gotta wash my hair every day, or it's like a fucking oil bath on my scalp. Just take it down and see."

I reached for the two sticks that were somehow the only thing keeping Rachel's long, thick hair in the bun.

"No." Rachel ducked away from me and gave me a stubborn look. "I'll wear your too-small shirt, but I'm keeping my hair up. My mom says it's not a flattering look when I wear my hair down."

"Yeah, well, your mom's a bitch, and we all know it."

Rachel didn't reply, and I kissed her cheek. "I'm sorry, sweetie. I didn't mean to upset you."

"You didn't. I know what my mom is."

We were silent for a moment, and then I put my arm around her and squeezed her tight. "You look beautiful, Rach. Now, let's go drink, dance, and make our men insane with lust."

"Sweetie, why don't we just go home?" I gave Rachel a worried look.

Three hours later, we were both standing in front of the sinks in the ladies' room at Ren's Bar.

She shook her head and finished washing her hands. "No, I'm fine."

"You're not fine."

"I am."

"He's an idiot, Rach."

She just shrugged, and I could see her blinking back the tears as she turned and reached for the paper towel.

Much to my confusion, Ren had not only not been sucked in by Rachel's gorgeous boobs, but he hadn't even spared a single glance at her all night. I'd sent her up twice to get fresh drinks instead of waiting for Liz to serve us, and each time, Ren had sent Peter, the other bartender, over to help her.

"Listen, why don't we return to my place and watch something loud and scary on Netflix? I'll make popcorn, and we'll forget all about -"

"No." Rachel turned back and adjusted her boobs before smiling weakly at me. "It's fine, Mads. Honest. It was stupid of me to think Ren might be interested in someone like me. Besides, Jacob hasn't even shown up yet. If we leave now, you'll never make him jealous enough to, uh, screw you tomorrow morning."

"I don't care," I said. "I'm not going to ask you to do something that makes you completely miserable."

"You're not," Rachel said. "We'd better get back out there. They're waiting for us."

"They can wait a little longer."

"They" were Elliott and Richie. Two guys around our age

and from the next town over. They had latched on to us about twenty minutes after we arrived at the bar. Elliott was polite and a little funny and obviously wanted to take Rachel home and do naughty things to her. Richie was an asswipe with an ego bigger than the damn planet.

My guy is kind of nice, right? Maybe I'll take him home and get him to-to pop my cherry tonight."

I frowned at her. "Rach, don't give it away to this guy just because he's nice, okay? You've waited this long, there's no reason to -"

"Exactly," Rachel reapplied her lip gloss, "I've waited too long, and I'm tired of being a virgin."

"But Ren -"

"What about him?" She gave me a furious look. "He doesn't want me, and it's stupid to wait to give my virginity to a guy who barely knows I exist. I'm glad your crush is working out for you, okay? I am. But mine isn't, and it's time I grew up and realized it."

"Okay."

She gave me another furious look before slumping against the counter. "I'm sorry."

"Don't be." I gave her a quick side-hug. "I get it. It's your body and your decision, and if you want to take Elliott home tonight and hump his nice-guy brains out, I support you."

She smiled a little. "Your guy is kind of a douchebag, honey."

"I know, right? Richie is a real piece of work, but honestly, it makes it a little easier. He's such an arrogant asshole that I don't feel bad just using him to make Jacob jealous."

I squeezed her again. "Ready to go back out there?"

"Yeah."

CHAPTER 6

Jacob

"Hi, handsome."

"Hi, Liz." I smiled politely at the dark-haired waitress. She had her hair in her usual pigtails, and I could see straight down her shirt when she leaned down. I kept my eyes on her face as a flash of disappointment crossed her face.

She straightened and placed one hand on her hip. "What can I get you?"

"Isn't this Madison's section?" Christ, did I have to sound so eager?

"She's not working tonight."

"What? She's not here?" I gave Liz a look of confusion.

"She's here, just not working. What can I get you to drink?"

"Uh, a beer. Whatever's on tap."

"Coming right up."

Liz walked away, and I stared around the bar. What the hell was going on? Madison wasn't working, but she was at the bar? I didn't see her, and I wondered for a minute if Liz was fucking with me.

"Holy shit." My gaze had landed on the hallway leading into the restrooms. Rachel Banks was walking out of the hallway and into the bar. Her hair was in its usual bun, and she was wearing a long skirt, but her shirt was incredibly tight and showed off a generous amount of her large tits. My gaze automatically went to the bar.

Maybe it was because I spent every Friday night in the damn bar, or maybe it was just because a man who had spent the last nine months lusting after a woman he could never have recognized another asshole who was in the same fucked-up situation, but I knew that Ren wanted Rachel as much as I wanted Madison.

Ren was staring at Rachel as she crossed the bar. I frowned in confusion. There was lust in Ren's gaze, plenty of it, but anger almost overshadowed it. Why would he be angry? Why would he be –

I forgot about Ren's anger as I caught sight of Madison walking behind Rachel. All the blood in my head drained to my dick, and it swelled with painful intensity. Her dark hair was down, and her shirt hugged her tits. She was wearing a short little skirt that barely covered her ass and showed off her smooth, pale legs. An image of those legs spread wide while I buried my face in her pussy, went through me, and I groaned at the pressure in my jeans. Fuck, I was going to explode.

I'd spent all week dreaming about Madison and wishing I could go to her. I had worked overtime at Eleanor's, both in a bid to keep myself too busy to think about Maddie and to finish the job so I didn't have to avoid Eleanor's goddamn wandering hands and come up with excuse after excuse about why I couldn't join her in her fucking bedroom. I had finished the job this afternoon, thank fucking Christ.

Maddie and Rachel sat at their table, and I suddenly understood Ren's anger. I was immediately filled with the same outrage when I saw the pimple-faced kid put his arm around my woman. Another dark-haired guy was grinning at Rachel, his gaze practically glued to her tits, but I didn't spare a thought for Ren or his rage. My own rage was threatening to spill out and send me on a rampage that would end with me kicking the shit out of a kid decades younger than me.

I tried to breathe deeply, but when the guy started to lean toward Madison, I was up and out of my seat. Before I could stomp over there, Liz stood in front of me.

"Here's your drink, sweetheart." She set it on the table.

"Thanks."

She smiled expectantly at me, and I yanked my wallet from my pocket and handed her a ten. "Keep the change."

"Why, thanks, big guy. Hey, what are you doing later tonight? You want to get a drink after my shift?" She smiled again at me, and I bared my teeth.

"Not fucking interested, Liz. Leave."

She took a step back. "You don't have to be a dick about it."

I ignored her. My hands clenched into fists when she finally left, and I could see the empty table where Mads had been sitting. I looked around the bar frantically. Ren was already out from behind the bar, and I strode across the room, following him to the small dance floor.

Dimly I was aware of Ren pushing the dark-haired guy away from Rachel and taking her by the arm, but most of my concentration was on Madison and the pimply dick holding her way too tight as they danced.

I stood behind Madison and glared at the guy. "Get lost, asshole."

"Who the fuck are you?" The kid gave me a look that was supposed to scare me.

I laughed in his face. "Get. Lost."

"You know this guy?" He asked Madison, and she nodded. "Tell him to fuck off then. We're dancing."

"Last chance, dickhead. Take your hands off of her."

"What if I don't?"

Madison squirmed out of his grip and put her arm around my waist. "C'mon, Jacob, let's go."

The guy glared at her. "Are you fucking kidding me? You've been wagging your ass and pussy at me all night, and now you're just going to -"

"You need to shut the fuck up right now." My voice wasn't loud, but the kid took one look at my face and stepped back.

"Fuck this shit. Elliott, get your whore and let's get the fuck out of here."

Madison turned to the dark-haired guy, her body tensing. "Where's Rachel? What did you do with Rachel?"

I put my arm around her and squeezed her hip. "She's with Ren."

"Are you sure?"

"Yes." I nodded toward the hallway, where Rachel disappeared with Ren into his office.

"Okay." Madison's body sagged with relief as Elliott rolled his eyes and followed his buddy off the dance floor.

Without speaking, I pulled Madison into my arms. I couldn't dance worth shit, but I could at least fucking sway to the music. Madison put her arms around my shoulders and smiled up at me.

"Hi."

"What are you doing, Madison?"

"What do you mean?"

"You show up at the bar in a skirt that barely covers your ass. Hell, half the guys in here have probably seen your goddamn panties, and you're flirting and dancing with some asshole."

"One – I'm not wearing panties, so there's no way anyone's seen them and – oh, hello, Mr. Jacob."

I growled at her as she rubbed against my obvious erection. "Stop it. And don't you dare leave the house again without panties. Do you hear me?"

"I'm wearing a bra," she said with a sassy grin.

I bit the inside of my cheek to stop from returning her grin. "I mean it, Madison. You wear your fucking panties whenever you leave the house."

"Why? What's the big deal?"

"Because I don't want anyone seeing what's -"

Shit. I couldn't say it. Not to her.

"Seeing what's yours?" She smiled at me and rubbed the back of my neck with her soft hand. "Is that what you were going to say?"

"No."

"Liar." She stood on her tiptoes and pressed her mouth against my ear. I should have been pushing her away, but instead, I just held her tighter against me.

She kissed my earlobe before licking the curve of it. "My pussy is yours, Jacob."

"It isn't." My voice was hoarse, on the breaking point of need.

"It is. Only yours. I'll never let anyone else fuck my little pussy but you. You know that, don't you?"

"Don't say that, baby."

"It's true. I'll wait for you forever if I have to."

"Mads…"

"Take me home, Jacob," she whispered into my ear. "Take me home so I can fuck you. It's what we both want, what we both need. Isn't it?"

"Yes." I was helpless to resist her. Powerless to ignore my need for her.

She kissed my cheek and took a step back. I immediately missed her softness and her warmth. She took my hand, and we were halfway across the bar when she stopped.

"What's wrong?" I was suddenly afraid she'd changed her mind.

"Rachel. I need to tell her I'm leaving with you, or she'll be worried." She turned and, still holding my hand, marched toward Ren's office. I followed her like an obedient puppy. Hell, I'd have been surprised if my tongue wasn't hanging out. I was pretty sure that half the goddamn patrons in the bar were staring at us, and I didn't give a fuck.

We walked down the hallway and Madison was just about to knock on Ren's door when the distinct sound of a woman moaning came drifting out of his office. She stared up at me, and we both leaned a little closer. There was more moaning and the gasps of a woman on the edge of her orgasm. The low sound of Ren's voice was too quiet to understand. Rachel's higher pitch was perfectly understandable.

"No one fucks me but you, Ren."

"Holy shit," Mads whispered. "Is that -"

She was cut off by the unmistakable cries of a woman coming and coming pretty fucking hard from the sounds of it. My cock hardened again. Soon it would be my woman making those noises as I fucked her over and over again.

"Jacob?" The look on Maddie's face was adorable. "Did Rachel just..."

"Have an orgasm?"

She nodded, and I grinned at her. "Yeah, sounded like it to me. C'mon, this isn't the time to interrupt. You can text her."

"Yeah, okay." Madison was still staring at the door and said almost absently, "That sounded like a really good one."

I tapped her on the ass and leaned down to suck on her earlobe. "Get your sweet ass in my truck, and I'll take you home and give you a dozen of those really good ones."

"Promise?" she said breathlessly.

"Yes."

"Can I sit on your face?" She gave me a sweet little smile, and I almost came in my pants.

"Fuck. Yes, you can sit on my face. Now let's go before I push you up against the wall, and Rachel gets to hear what you sound like when you're coming."

"Yes, Jacob."

I grinned at her, and we walked quickly out of the bar and into the cool night air. We were at my truck, and I was unlocking the door when Mads made a low gasp.

"What's wrong?"

"It's Rachel."

I followed her gaze. Rachel was hurrying to her car. Her hair was down, and I was surprised to see it hung nearly to her waist. I'd never seen her hair down before.

"Give me one minute, okay?" Madison said.

I nodded and waited at the truck as she hurried across the parking lot to Rachel. I watched the two women talk. After nearly five minutes, Madison hugged Rachel, and the curvier woman climbed into her car. She drove away as Madison walked back to me.

"Everything okay?"

"Yeah, I think so." Madison was chewing on her bottom lip, and I squeezed her hand.

"If you need to be with your friend tonight, I understand."

She smiled at me. "Thank you, but Rachel said she wanted to be alone."

"Did Ren…"

She hesitated and then said, "Rachel's, um, a virgin and Ren knew it somehow. I guess he went all alpha male and told her that her cherry belonged to him and she wasn't allowed to let another guy even touch her. They didn't fuck or anything, but he made her come."

"So, why is she leaving?" I asked.

She said he went all weird as soon as she climaxed and told her that she should leave."

"He's older than her. Maybe the age difference freaks him out."

She gave me a wry look. "Not that big of an age difference, and besides, just because it's your hang-up doesn't mean it's Ren's."

"Are you sure you still want to do this?" I asked.

She ran her hand over my flat stomach, and my cock surged against my jeans. "Are you trying to get out of your promise to let me sit on your face, Jacob?"

"No," I said. "But -"

"Then take me home so you can eat my pussy."

I unlocked the truck and lifted her into it.

"You should know I might ruin your seats," she said when I slid behind the wheel. "Between listening to Ren make Rachel come and knowing that you're going to eat my pussy, I'm soaking wet."

"The seats are leather, don't worry about it." I lifted the divider and patted the spot beside me. "Slide over beside me."

She did what I asked, and I started the truck and drove out of the parking lot. "Lift your skirt and show me your sweet pussy."

"Yes, Jacob."

I bit back my groan at her obedience. She wiggled her skirt up to her waist, and when I stopped at a red light, I studied her pussy in the dim light. "Spread your legs."

She spread her legs, and I squeezed her knee. "Rub your pussy for me."

She dipped her hand between her legs and moaned when she made contact with her pussy.

"You nice and wet for me, baby?"

"Yes."

"Show me."

She lifted her hand, and I stared at her wet fingers before opening my mouth. She stuck her fingers in my mouth, and I licked them clean as the light turned green. "You taste so good, baby."

"Thank you, Jacob."

"I can't wait to have my tongue buried nice and deep in your tight little hole. Is that what you want?"

"Yes." She said it with a moan. Her fingers were back in her pussy, and I could see her rubbing furiously at her clit.

"Stop it, baby."

"No!" She pouted at me, and I squeezed her knee.

"No coming yet."

"I want to."

"I know. But be my good girl and keep your fingers out of your pussy."

She pouted again but moved her fingers away.

"Good girl. Keep your legs spread nice and wide for me."

"Will you put your fingers in me, Jacob?"

"We're almost home."

"I need something in my pussy." She gave me a pleading look. "I can't stand how empty it feels."

"You can't come. Do you understand?"

"Yes," she said eagerly. "I won't come, Jacob. I promise."

I reached down and cupped her pussy. She was soaking wet, and I gave her clit a little rub before sinking two fingers into her tight pussy. She squealed happily and clenched around me. When she started to hump my hand, I shook my head.

"No, baby. Don't fuck my fingers."

"Please?"

"No. Stay still, or I'll take my fingers out and then your little pussy won't have anything."

She moaned and grabbed my wrist, keeping my fingers embedded deep inside of her. I could feel her pussy clenching and unclenching around me, and I grinned as I turned onto her street. "You like having my fingers inside you, baby?"

"I want your cock in my pussy."

"Soon." I parked in her driveway and pulled my fingers free. I licked them clean and shut off the truck. I waited a beat and then stared at her. "Madison, are you sure – absolutely sure – that this is what you want?"

"I've never been more sure of anything in my life." She took my hand and kissed the palm of it before smiling her sweet smile. "Come inside, Jacob. Make me yours."

CHAPTER 7

Madison

I didn't get nervous until we were both in my bedroom. Suddenly, the room seemed too warm, and my hands were getting clammy. I didn't know why I was nervous. I'd already had sex with Jacob and had his cock in my mouth, for God's sake.

"Baby, what's wrong?" Jacob was studying me carefully.

Afraid he would call a stop to everything if he knew I was suddenly nervous, I smiled and lied. "Nothing's wrong."

He stepped forward and pulled me into his embrace. His big hands rubbed my lower back. "Don't lie to me, Madison. I don't ever want you to lie to me. Okay?"

"Okay."

He smoothed my hair back from my face. "Now, tell me what's wrong."

"I'm just suddenly feeling a little nervous. I don't know why I'm nervous, but I don't want you to leave. Okay?"

"I won't leave. Do you want to just lie on the bed together?"

My mouth dropped open, and I started to giggle. "Jacob Marken, did you just ask me if I want to cuddle?"

His cheeks went red, and I wrapped my arms around his waist and squeezed hard before rubbing myself against his erection. "You're amazing. Your dick is rock fucking hard, and you're willing to just cuddle with me."

He cleared his throat. "I don't want to push you into anything you don't -"

"I want this. I want this very much. I just realized that we haven't even kissed yet, and, I don't know, it made me feel weird."

He smiled at me before cupping my face and lowering his mouth to mine. At the first touch of his firm lips. I moaned and parted mine. He didn't tease or torment. He slid his tongue into my mouth and kissed me like I belonged to him.

I returned his kiss with an eagerness that should have been embarrassing but wasn't. Jacob was a fantastic kisser, and I could have spent the next decade just kissing him. When his big hand cupped my breast, I wished desperately that I wasn't wearing a bra. I rubbed up against him as he kneaded my breast, his thumb rubbing my hardening nipple.

"Jacob, please," I whimpered against his mouth.

He stepped away from me and pulled my shirt over my head. He reached behind me and unhooked my bra, giving my breasts a look of pure appreciation when he took my bra off. "So beautiful, Mads."

"Thank you."

He unzipped my skirt and tugged it down my legs. "Step out."

I stepped out of the skirt, and he studied my naked body before leaning down and kissing me again. I sucked on his tongue when he slid it into my mouth and tried to cling to him when he pulled back. "Lie on the bed, baby."

I did what he asked, watching with barely controlled lust as he stripped off his clothing. It was the first time I'd seen him completely naked, and I studied him with a lack of inhibition as he stood in my room. His upper body was just as gorgeous as I remembered with his broad shoulders, flat stomach and dark hair that I was almost desperate to touch. He had a narrow waist and hips with muscular thighs and calves. My gaze arrowed in on his cock. It was fully erect, the head a dark red and already dripping pre-cum. It was long and thick and mine.

All mine.

When he stretched out on his side beside me, I pouted at him again. "You said I could sit on your face."

"Soon. I want those pretty little nipples in my mouth first."

My nipples were already hard, and I moaned when he leaned down and circled them with his tongue. My hands threaded through his thick hair, and I pulled hard. He growled against my breast and nipped the side of it. I squealed and eased my grip as he said, "Be my good girl."

"Yes, Jacob."

That made him groan, and he sucked hard on my nipple. My back arched, and I cried his name. The suction of his mouth, the way his tongue brushed back and forth over the tip of my nipple, was making me crazy. When he switched to the other one and tormented it, I pounded on his back and pleaded for mercy.

He raised his head and grinned at me while his fingers pinched and toyed with my sensitive nipples. "I love your nipples. They're so fucking sensitive."

"Jacob, please."

"Please, what?"

"I need to come."

"Soon." He dipped his head and went back to work teasing my nipples. His big thigh pushed between my legs, and I humped it shamelessly, rubbing my clit against him in a desperate attempt to come.

He pulled on my nipple with his teeth. I squeaked and froze against him. He released it and licked away the slight sting. "I said no coming, Mads."

"You're the worst!" I smacked him on the back, and he laughed before rubbing his hair-roughened thigh against my pussy. I moaned and clutched at his back, wanting to rub myself against him but not quite daring to, with his lips still attached to my nipple.

"Do you want to sit on my face now, baby?"

"Yes."

"Not yet."

"Goddamn you!"

He laughed again and continued his torment to my nipples. This time, he pushed his hand between my thighs and lightly stroked the lips of my pussy. "You're so wet for me. Me and only me, isn't that right?"

"Yes, Jacob."

His fingers brushed my clit, and I shrieked and arched into him. He immediately withdrew his hand, and I made a sharp cry of need. "Jacob!"

"Shh, baby. I want you to come while I'm licking your little pussy."

"Then let me sit on your goddamn face!"

"All right."

"No! Stop teasing me and...what?"

"I said, all right." He flipped to his back and grinned at me. "Hop on, baby."

He didn't have to tell me a third time. I scrambled up and straddled his face a bit awkwardly but enthusiastically. His big hands curled around my thighs, and he tugged me a little closer before inhaling. "You smell so sweet."

I moaned when his tongue flicked out and licked my pussy lips. "You taste sweet, baby."

"Please," I whispered. My brash, take-charge personality was gone. One stroke of Jacob's tongue and I was already reduced to a whimpering, pleading mess. "Oh please, taste me."

"Whatever you want, baby." He licked my lips again, and I shuddered all over before grabbing the headboard. My knuckles went white as Jacob licked away all my juices. He was deliberately avoiding my clit, but when I tried to grind my pussy against his mouth, his big hands around my thighs stopped me.

His hot, wet tongue licked lower, and when he pushed it into my hole, I began to beg mindlessly. He pushed it in and out, and fuck, it felt fantastic, but my clit was throbbing with an almost painful intensity.

"Please," I begged as I rocked against his face, "please, my clit!"

"What about it, baby?" Jacob's voice was muffled, and just the way his lips moved against my heated flesh made me want to scream.

"Please lick it."

His warm laugh vibrated against my pussy, and I cried out when he made a slow lick from the bottom of my pussy right to the bottom of my clit. I squeezed the headboard again and made an inarticulate noise of pure lust. If he didn't lick my clit soon, if he didn't give me relief for –

I screamed, my back arching when Jacob's hot tongue licked across my clit. My orgasm shot through me like a bullet, making my body shake and my pussy gush all over Jacob's mouth and face. He licked my clit again as the pleasure crested inside of me. I couldn't help it. I screamed again, grinding my pussy against Jacob's lips and tongue. He sucked at my clit, sending little aftershocks of pleasure tingling through me. I jerked and twitched, my grip on the headboard the only thing keeping me upright.

"Move down, baby."

"Can't...let go. Fall...over," I gasped.

He chuckled, and his hands moved to my waist. "You can. I'll help you."

I let go of the headboard, but before I could tip over, Jacob was holding me upright and helping me to ease down his broad body. I straddled his thighs, my body still shaking and twitching from my climax, as Jacob kept one hand on my waist and used the other to wipe his face with the sheet.

"I'm sorry," I said.

He shook his head. "Don't ever be sorry for coming on my face. In fact, if you're not coming on my face once a day, we're doing something wrong."

I grinned weakly at him. I was tired and more than a little sleepy, but Jacob was hard as a rock. "Are you going to fuck me now?"

"Yes, baby, I am."

"Okay." I gave him a pleased little smile that made him grin.

"Can you ride me, Mads?"

I nodded, and he helped me move forward and then guide his dick to the entrance of my pussy. The head was an even darker red and slick with precum. It brushed against my pussy, and both of us groaned.

"Fuck, get me inside of you before I come all over your fucking pussy."

I pushed down, feeling the broad head parting my folds and sliding into my hole. I tried to stop halfway, to give my pussy a chance to adjust, but Jacob shook his head. "No, don't stop."

"It's too big," I complained. "Just give me a minute to -"

"No." His big hands cupped my hips in a hard grip, and he thrust upwards, forcing my pussy to take another few inches. "Take my cock, Madison."

Shit. His demand shouldn't have turned me on so much. But there was no denying it did. I pushed against him, and we both watched as my pussy took inch after inch of his thick cock until he was seated entirely inside of me.

"Oh God," I moaned.

Jacob reached up and cupped my tits, playing with my nipples. "Move, Maddie. Fuck my dick."

I braced my hands on his chest, touching the rough hair with the pads of my fingers before I began to move. I slid up and down his cock with slow, deliberate movements, keeping my gaze on his face.

"Good, baby. That's so good. Your little pussy feels like heaven around my dick. Did you know that?"

"No," I moaned.

"It does. So good. You're mine, Madison. You belong to me. Say it."

"I belong to you."

"That's right, you do. Your little pussy is mine now. Mine to fuck, mine to taste, mine to – oh fuck, yeah, that's good, baby. Do that again."

I rotated my hips in a slow spiral as I pushed down on his cock again. He groaned, and his entire body jerked. "Fuck, I'm gonna come if you keep doing that."

"I want you to," I whispered. "I want you to come in me, Jacob."

"I want that too, baby. But you gotta come again for me first. Rub your pussy for me. Show me your clit."

I leaned back, bracing one hand on his raised knees for support and using my other to rub my pussy. I plucked at my clit and was surprised at how sensitive it still was, at how quickly I was almost to another climax.

"That's right. Rub it again for me, baby. Show me how pretty you look when you're coming on my cock." Jacob was holding my waist again, his hips thrusting with slow and steady strokes as I rubbed and pulled on my clit.

"Pinch it for me, baby."

I pinched, crying out at the sensation as Jacob made a hard thrust.

"Good. Do it again."

"I'll come if I do," I panted.

"That's what I want. Remember? I want you to come on my cock."

His hips were moving fast now, his dick so hard and thick inside of me that I could feel my inner walls still trying to stretch to accommodate his width. I circled my clit with trembling fingers as Jacob moved even faster. My desire was growing, the pleasure coiling in my belly until I was shaking with my need for relief.

"Do it, baby. Right now."

I pinched my clit just as Jacob reached up and pinched my right nipple. Pleasure roared through me, and I clenched around his cock as I rubbed furiously at my clit.

"Fuck!" Jacob shouted hoarsely, his hand dropping to my hip as he thrust up so deep that I felt a brief flash of pain. "Oh fuck!"

His big body shook, and he bellowed another curse before he came inside me. My pussy milked him instinctively, pulling his seed deep inside of me as he came and came again. I rode out his orgasm, watching the pleasure dance across his face until he collapsed below me. He was panting hard, and I pressed my hand against his heart. It was beating like an out-of-control racehorse, and I gave him an alarmed look.

"Jacob? Are you okay?"

"Unfuckingbelievable, Mads."

I giggled and climbed off of him. His cum was starting to drip down my leg, but Jacob shook his head and pulled me against his side when I tried to climb out of bed. "Stay right here."

"I need to clean up," I protested. "There's like a gallon of sperm coming out of me."

He laughed, and I shivered all over when he reached between my legs. His fingers came back dripping, and he gave me a satisfied smile. "I don't think I've ever come so hard in my life, Mads."

"You're welcome."

He laughed and pulled me closer, kissing the top of my head. We were silent for a while, and I was almost asleep when he said, "He would hate me for this."

I sat up, knowing exactly who he was talking about. "He wouldn't, Jacob. He loved you. You were his best friend."

I could see the sorrow on his face, and I rubbed his chest. "Honey, he wouldn't hate you. He would be surprised, maybe, but ultimately he'd be happy for us."

"You don't know that."

"I do. You might have been his best friend, but he was my dad. I knew him better than anyone else. What he wanted was for me to be happy. You make me happy. I've loved you since I was fifteen, Jacob Marken."

"I know."

I blushed a little. "Was I that obvious?"

He just shrugged. "I swear I didn't think of you as anything more than Frank's daughter until…"

"Until the night of his funeral."

"Yeah." He studied me for a moment. "Since that night, I haven't stopped thinking about you. I haven't been with a woman for over a year. All I want is you. I love you. You're mine now. Do you understand that?"

I nodded. "Yes. It's what I want. To be yours…forever."

I leaned over him and kissed him on the mouth. "Forever, Jacob. And not that I'm complaining, but why the sudden change of heart? Last weekend, you were telling me how wrong it was."

He studied me for a moment. "I can't resist you anymore, and I'm tired of trying. Do I still think your dad would beat the hell out of me if he were alive? Yeah, but it doesn't change how I feel about you. I need you. I can't live without you, Maddie."

He cupped my face and gave me a rough kiss. "It's not going to be easy. People are going to talk about us. You know that, right?"

"Let them talk. I don't care what they say."

"As soon as you're finished school, we'll get married. That'll shut them up."

"You- you want to marry me?"

"Mine forever, Mads. I wasn't joking about that. After we're married, you can do your dental hygienist thing for a few years before I knock you up."

I blinked at him. "I – pregnant?"

"You don't want kids?"

"No, I do. I love kids. I just – you want me to have your baby?"

He grinned at me. "I want you to have six of my babies."

"Um, we need to negotiate that. I'm not having six kids."

"Five?"

"Two."

"Four?"

"Three, maybe."

He gave me a contented look. "Three is a good number. I love you, Mads."

I relaxed against him, resting my head on his chest and listening to the steady beat of his heart. "I love you too, Jacob."

THE BARTENDER

THE BARTENDER

WORKING MEN SERIES BOOK THREE

By Ramona Gray

He goes down better than a shot of whiskey.

Rachel

Being a twenty-three-year-old virgin isn't the worst thing in the world.

Being a twenty-three-year-old virgin in love with a man who doesn't know I exist?

Tragic, right?

Local bartender Ren Parker might not be into librarians with questionable fashion taste, but it doesn't stop me from fantasizing about getting him alone in the library and breaking all the rules about quiet time.

But a girl has to be realistic, and I can't stay a virgin forever. Picking up a nice guy at the bar to take my V-card is surprisingly easy. That is until Ren discovers what I'm doing. Suddenly, the man I thought wouldn't give me the time of day has his hands all over me until my insides are shaken and stirred.

He says my virginity belongs to him, and I'm more than happy to prove him right.

Ren

I've wanted Rachel Banks from the moment I saw her. Sweet and gorgeous with a body I can't wait to have under me, she's got my world turned upside down.

But a man like me isn't meant to have a woman like her. Until the night I see her about to give away what's mine.

Now, I'm insisting she belongs to me and I won't rest until she gives me her innocence and her heart. I'm playing a dangerous game. I have a past that a woman like Rachel would never understand, and the right thing to do is let a better man have her.

Too bad I've never been good at giving up what's mine.

CHAPTER 1

Rachel

"**M**s. Banks, I can't find the book."

I moved around the desk and followed the little girl across the library to the children's section. "It's supposed to be right here, but it isn't."

I scanned the shelf before studying the one above it. "Here it is, Emily. It just got shelved wrong."

"Isn't it your job to shelve it right?" The seven-year-old cocked her eyebrow at me, and I swallowed down my urge to laugh.

"Everyone makes mistakes."

"I guess." She took the book and then smiled at me. "Sorry, Ms. Banks. I wasn't trying to be mean. You're a real good librarian."

"Thank you, Emily.

"Emily? Em! C'mon, let's go. Mom's waiting for us in the

car." Her older brother, Ethan, was waving at her from across the library. "C'mon, dummy!"

"Be quiet, Ethan!" Emily yelled. "You're not supposed to yell in the library!"

"You're yelling, too!"

Emily gave me a do-you-see-how-I-suffer look before marching toward the desk. "I just gotta check this book out, and then I'm ready."

Ethan tossed the football he was holding into the air and caught it. "Fine. I'm gonna go wait in the car with Mom."

Emily waited patiently as I scanned her card and book into the system. I tucked a bookmark into the book and handed it to her. "Remember, it's due back in fourteen days."

"I know. Hey, Ms. Banks?"

"Yes?"

"Why aren't you married? Is it because you're a librarian?"

"Why would you think that?"

She shrugged. "Ethan says that librarians never get married. They just go to work and sit at home with their twelve cats. Do you have a cat, Ms. Banks?"

"No, I'm allergic. And not being married doesn't have anything to do with being a librarian. Plenty of librarians are married, Emily."

"Okay." She turned and walked away, apparently having lost interest in why I wasn't married.

I watched her go, a small smile on my face, before glancing around the library. For a Saturday afternoon, it was surprisingly empty. Typically, Saturday was our busiest day. A group of seniors usually met after lunch to read the magazines and gossip quietly. The computer room was almost always full, and there was usually a table or two of students, with their textbooks, tablets, and laptops covering most of the table.

This afternoon, only three people were in the computer room, the seniors had never shown up, and half a dozen people perused the books. I walked to the cart of books at the end of the biography aisle and began to shelve them.

Your virginity is mine, Rachel. Mine to take, mine to own.

I whirled around, my heart thudding in my chest. There was no one behind me. His deep voice was just in my head. The way it had been nearly every hour since I'd left Ren's Bar last night. Driving me insane. Making me lose sleep and not eat and shelve the damn books wrong. It was stupid even to think he was here. He *never* came to the library.

I shook my head to clear it and shelved the book I was holding before grabbing another.

No one looks at you, no one touches you, no one fucks you but me. Is that clear, sweetheart? Say it.

"No one fucks me but you, Ren," I murmured before looking around. Thank God there was no one near me. I rested my burning forehead against the shelf of books. The temptation to go back, to relive that moment from last night, was too hard to resist. I closed my eyes and let it consume me.

"YOU'RE GORGEOUS. YOU KNOW THAT, RIGHT?" ELLIOTT WAS holding me too tightly as we danced, his gaze glued to my exposed cleavage.

I tried to wiggle back a little. I was starting to regret coming to the bar tonight. I had gone to Ren's bar for two reasons. One – to support my best friend Madison, who was trying to make her crush jealous and two – to try and make *my* crush jealous. I had failed miserably at it. Despite dressing sexier than I usually did – okay, maybe that was an exaggeration. I was still wearing my hair up in a bun, and my tights and ankle-length skirt completely covered my round ass and chunky thighs. But, I had let Madison convince me to wear a shirt that was four sizes too small and barely covered my breasts.

Anyway, it was a waste of energy. I'd been lusting after Ren Parker for months. I'd even had the silly idea that he would be the one I'd give my virginity to, even though he'd never once looked at me like he wanted me. So, when Madison told me of her plan to make Jacob jealous, I temporarily lost my mind and decided to try the same thing with Ren.

Only it hadn't – wasn't – working. Whenever I went to Ren's bar, he usually at least acknowledged me, but tonight, he hadn't looked at me once. It was like he was deliberately avoiding me. I shouldn't have been as hurt as I was. I don't think I'd had a single conversation with the man beyond, "Hi. Nice weather, huh?" but I was hurt.

Hurt enough that I decided I was taking Elliott home and using him to get rid of my pesky virginity once and for all. I was twenty-three years old, and still being a virgin was starting to be embarrassing. I was self-conscious about my looks, but Elliott seemed to be a boob guy. Maybe he'd be so busy with them that he wouldn't notice how round my stomach was or how thick my thighs were.

Of course, now I was second-guessing my decision to screw Elliott. It wasn't just the way he couldn't stop leering at my breasts. It was his bad breath, his blank look when I'd asked him what his favourite book was, the erection he wasn't even trying to disguise as we danced. Did I want to give up my V-card to someone who didn't even read for pleasure?

Ren liked to read. I'd never seen him at the library, but I'd seen him with a book at the coffee shop a few times. A real book. Not a tablet or an e-reader, but a paper book. It was totally snobby of me, but knowing that he liked reading and reading paper books made me even more attracted. Like, wet in the pussy, tingly in the nipples, attracted to him.

What can I say? Hot guys who read turn me on.

"Did you hear me?" Elliott asked

I tried to smile. "Uh, thanks for the compliment. Do you think you could stop holding me so – oh!"

My arm was taken in a firm grip and I was pulled away from Elliott so hard that I stumbled in my sensible heels. I stared at the man holding my arm. "Ren? What are you doing?"

"You're touching what's mine." Ren wasn't even looking at me. He glared daggers at Elliott, and the younger man immediately stepped back, holding up his hands.

"Hey, she never said she had a guy."

"I don't," I said. "He's not my -"

"Hush, Rachel."

I hushed. It wasn't so much what Ren said but how he said it. I wasn't one for blind obedience to a man, but the tone of Ren's voice had me shutting my mouth with a snap.

"You don't ever touch her again. Do you understand?"

"Yeah, I get it," Elliott said a bit sullenly.

"Let's go," Ren said to me.

"Go where?"

He didn't reply, just started off the dance floor. He was still holding my arm, and I had no choice but to follow him. Out of the corner of my eye, I could see Jacob standing behind Madison. Ren was leading me into his office, and just before he closed the door, I saw Madison put her arm around Jacob's waist.

The door shut, and Ren dropped my arm. His office was

small, and Ren was a big man. I backed up nervously when he stepped toward me, but my butt hit the edge of his desk almost immediately, and I was trapped.

"What are you doing, Rachel?"

"Wh-what do you mean?"

"This." One finger brushed against the exposed swell of my right breast, and I moaned. I couldn't help it.

He gave me a hard grin. "Why are you showing off what belongs to me?"

"I – what?"

"These. Belong. To. Me." With a quick flick of his fingers, he flicked open the button that was straining to stay closed over my breasts. My shirt gaped open, and I automatically lifted my arms to cover my breasts.

"No." He blocked my attempt. "Arms at your side, sweetheart."

My arms dropped, and he studied my breasts, barely covered by my bright red bra. It was a demi-cup with lace edging, and he traced the edging with his fingers. "Your tits belong to me. Stay it, Rachel."

I shook my head mutely, but I didn't even try to stop him when he tugged on the edges of both cups of my bra. My nipples popped out like they'd been waiting all night for him. He made a low noise in the back of his throat that made my lower muscles clench and my pussy flutter.

"My nipples. Say it."

"No, I can't say that. I can't – ohh!"

He pulled on my nipples, forcing me to move closer to him as pain and pleasure flooded my body.

"Mine." His voice was matter-of-fact. His mouth came crashing down on mine before I could protest. My lips parted for his tongue, and I stood stock-still for a moment.

Ren was kissing me. Ren has his tongue in my mouth like he owned it. Ren was cupping my breasts and rubbing my nipples, and holy mother of Mary, it was the hottest moment of my life.

I threw my arms around his shoulders and pressed up against him. His long fingers tugged down my bra cups until my large breasts were completely exposed. He tugged at my nipples again as he angled his mouth over mine and kissed me deep. I let him take what he wanted from me, rubbing myself like an eager little slut against his obvious erection.

He pulled back, and I shuddered all over at the look in his eyes. He was usually so calm, so laid-back and almost sweet. There was nothing sweet in his gaze now.

"These are my tits." He gave them a hard squeeze. "Say it."

"They're yours." My voice was a whisper but steady enough.

"That's right, sweetheart. And are you going to show them to anyone else?"

"No."

"Good. I'm the only one who gets to see your tits."

"Okay." I wanted him to rub my nipples again, but he frowned and gave them a little pinch.

"Say it, Rachel."

"You're the only one who gets to see them."

"Why?"

"Because they're yours."

"That's right." He turned me around to face the desk with a swiftness that surprised me.

I ground my ass against his erection, and he pinched my nipples again. "Be good, sweetheart." He kissed my neck before sucking lightly. "Do you have any idea how tempted I am to mark your soft skin? To send you back out in the bar with my teeth marks all over your throat so that everyone knows you're mine?"

"Ren, please. I – I should go." I was so turned on the crotch of my panties was soaking wet. I decided it was probably better to get out of his office before he figured out how hot his claim of ownership was making me.

I realized with horror that he was pushing his hand under the waistband of my skirt. As it slid into my tights and panties, I tried to wrench away. "Ren, wait."

"No." Just that one word made my pussy clench. His foot kicked my legs apart, and then his hand was cupping my pussy. For the first time in my life, a hand other than my own was touching my pussy.

I froze against him as he made a low chuckle, and his other hand cupped my breast. "Look how wet you are for me."

"Ren, I… oh my God!"

His rough fingertips had found my swollen clit, and I shamefully began to writhe and beg immediately. "Please, oh please."

"You want to come, sweetheart?"

"Yes."

"Who else has touched you like this? Who else has made you come on their fingers?"

"N-no one."

"Good." The pleased tone in his voice made me gush liquid into his hand. "We're going to keep it that way. No one ever touches your pussy, but me. Do you understand? "

"Yes," I moaned. "No one touches me but you."

"Well done, sweetheart. Now just a few more," he paused and ran the tip of one finger against the side of my clit, "clarifications, and then I'll let you come. Okay?"

"Okay," I panted. I wiggled against Ren's hand, trying to move his fingers against my clit, and he gave my wet pussy lips a little slap that sent lightning bolts of pleasure up and down my spine.

"Stop trying to get off, sweetheart, and pay attention."

"Please," I moaned.

"Pay attention." He reached up and plucked the two sticks from my hair. My hair fell out of the bun, and he made a low noise of appreciation. "So pretty. I love your hair, sweetheart." He petted the long strands before burying his face in it and breathing deeply.

"Thank you," I whispered. "Please, can I come now?"

His fingers, his deliciously rough fingers, were still circling my clit. "Soon. Listen carefully, Rachel. Are you listening?"

"Yes." I arched my back, straining into his touch, when he cupped my breast again.

"Your virginity is mine, Rachel. Mine to take, mine to own."

I stiffened against him, and he made a soothing noise before gently caressing my breast. "It's mine. Do you agree?"

"Ren, I – oh, oh my gosh!"

His fingers were rubbing my clit again, and I was on the verge of my climax when he stopped.

"No!" I was almost crying for my relief, my body shaking and my nipples so hard they were painful.

"Do you agree, Rachel?"

"Yes," I moaned, "yes, my virginity is yours."

"Good, sweetheart."

"Please touch me."

"No one looks at you, no one touches you, no one fucks you but me. Is that clear, sweetheart? Say it."

"No one fucks me but you, Ren." At that point, I would have opened the door and shouted it to the entire bar if he'd asked me to.

His fingers pinched my clit, pinched and then pulled, and I cried out as my climax washed over me like a tidal wave. My body shook, my knees buckled, and I would have fallen to the floor if Ren hadn't held me up with an arm around my waist. I shuddered and moaned as Ren slid his hand free.

"Bend over, sweetheart." He pressed on my lower back, and I bent over the desk obediently, my breasts pressing against the smooth wood. Ren pulled up my skirt, and I stared wide-eyed at the wall. Holy shit. I was about to have sex with Ren Parker. He was going to take my virginity and –

"Fuck."

My skirt was almost over my ass, and I looked over my shoulder in confusion when Ren tugged it back down. "Ren?"

"Stand up."

I straightened. My legs shook, and I weaved slightly when he turned me around. Regret, lust and what looked like anger crossed his face as he quickly popped my breasts back into my bra and buttoned my shirt again. He scowled at how much of my breasts were still showing before reaching down and adjusting his cock.

"Ren? What's wrong?"

"Nothing. You need to go home."

"What?" I stared at him in numb disbelief. "No, wait. I – aren't we going to have sex?"

He shook his head, and I chewed on my bottom lip. "But you said my virginity was yours."

His groan and the way he clenched his fists only confused me more. "You need to leave, Rachel."

"I don't understand. What did I do wrong? If you tell me what I did wrong, I won't do it again."

"No, it's not..." His gaze drifted to my breasts again, and he reached down and adjusted his cock again. "For Christ's sake, Rachel. Will you just please do what I say and go the fuck home?"

Hurt flooded through me, and I turned and fled his office.

CHAPTER 2

Ren

"You gonna tell me what the fuck is wrong or just sit there and pout all goddamn night?"

My gaze slid to the woman sitting on Jack's lap. She studied me for a moment before pressing a kiss against Jack's mouth. "I'm going to have a bath."

She slid off his lap, twitching a little when Jack gave her ass a squeeze, and smiled at me. "It was nice to meet you formally, Ren."

"You too, Lily."

I watched Jack watch her ass sway out of the living room and grinned at him when he finally turned his attention back to me. "Never thought a woman would tame you."

Jack shrugged and took a swig of beer. "What can I say? She's got me wrapped around her fucking baby finger…and she don't even know it."

An orange tabby wandered into the living room. It fixed

me with a look, found me wanting, and ambled to Jack. A rumbling purr came from its chest as it brushed repeatedly against Jack's legs. My jaw dropped when it jumped into his lap, and Jack petted it roughly.

"What the fuck happened to you?"

Jack arched his eyebrows at me. "What's that supposed to mean?"

"I mean, for the last month, you've been playing house with Lily "Ice Queen" Carson, and you got a damn cat in your lap."

"I like pussy."

I snorted and took a swallow of beer. "Are you and the Ice Queen serious?"

"Her name is Lily, not Ice Queen, and yeah, we are."

"What the fuck have you done with my best friend?" I rested my beer on my knee.

"Oh please, you tryin' to tell me that if that sugar-won't-melt-in-her-mouth librarian offered up her virginal pussy on a platter, you wouldn't be following her around like a dog with your tongue out? I got me a woman that I love. End of story."

I peeled off a section of the label on my bottle. "You know I'm happy for you, right?"

"Yeah. Thanks, brother."

I ripped off another layer of label. Jack Williams was the closest thing to family I had. I'd moved here nearly six years ago, determined to start fresh and leave my past behind me. Not two months after I moved here, my shitbucket of a car had crapped out on me. I'd taken it to the mechanic in town – Jack's father.

Jack's old man had been an asshole, but Jack was a good guy, despite his fuck-you attitude and his occasional dickish behaviour. It was Jack who had gotten a bunch of his high-school buddies to help me renovate the bar after I bought it three years ago.

Hell, it was Jack who had convinced the bank to give me the loan to *buy* the bar. I'd grown up in the city, and the everyone-knows-everyone small town vibe was as foreign to me as streets lined with skyscrapers were to Jack. The bank manager had owed Jack a favour from high school, and Jack had finally cashed it in to help me.

After years of watching my back and never trusting anyone but myself, it was an almost unfathomable act of kindness.

"So, are you gonna tell me what's wrong, or do I have to stare at your ugly face all fucking night?" Jack asked.

I rolled the bit of label stuck to my fingers into a tiny ball. "I fucked up with Rachel."

"Oh yeah?" Jack rubbed the cat's scarred ears affectionately. "You tell her goodbye instead of hello when you bumped into her on the street?"

I rolled my eyes when Jack laughed. "What? It could be that. Her little pussy has you so worked up, you don't know if you're comin' or goin'. Although the way you've been lustin' after the sweet little librarian for the last three years, I imagine you're doin' a lot of comin'. Am I right?"

He made a jacking off motion that I ignored. "I told Rachel that her virginity was mine and that no one else was allowed to touch her. Then I made her come all over my fingers in my goddamn office."

Jack leaned forward, and the cat made an irritated meow and jumped off his lap. "Holy fucking shit. You are fucking kidding me."

I shook my head. "I wish I was. She came into the bar Friday night with Madison. She was wearing this shirt that –

that showed off her tits, and she was dancing with this guy, and I lost my fucking mind."

"Hold up. Rachel Banks was showing off her tits? Seriously? The woman dresses like a virginal librarian."

"She is a virginal librarian."

"Is she actually a virgin, though? I know everyone thinks she is, but -"

"She is." My cock twitched against my jeans. "I was ninety-eight percent certain before Friday night, and now I'm a hundred percent."

"You popped her cherry?"

I shook my head. "No. But she didn't correct me when I told her it belonged to me. She even admitted that no one had touched her pussy but me."

"Jesus." Jack leaned back in his chair. "How the fuck that hot piece of ass has gone this long without even having her pussy touched, I'll never know. She tries to hide it with her clothes, but that body of hers is -"

"Enough." My temper was rising. I knew Jack had no interest in Rachel, but the anger was still there. "Don't talk about her body."

Jack gave me an assessing look. "Keep your dick in your pants. I ain't after your girl."

"She's not mine."

Jack laughed and drank some beer. "You're fighting a losing battle, brother."

"I'm not. Do I want her? Yeah, maybe a little, but that doesn't mean I -"

"A little? When was the last time you fucked a woman?"

"What's that have to do with anything?"

"When?"

I sighed. "Two years ago."

"Fuck me."

"No thanks."

Jack stretched his legs out. "Two years is a long time to go without some pussy."

Yeah, it fucking was, but only Rachel had done it for me for a very long time. I drank almost half my beer in two big swallows. I couldn't tell Jack that the last two women I'd slept with had looked eerily similar to Rachel. He'd think I'd lost my damn mind.

Fuck. I *had* lost my damn mind.

"If you made her come, then obviously she's into you. Why are you fucking sitting here at my house instead of getting with her?" Jack asked.

"It's Monday night. She's working until seven."

Jack checked his watch. "So, in half an hour, you go to the library, drive your woman home, and fuck the virgin right out of her."

"I can't."

"Can't or won't?"

"She's too good for me. I don't deserve -"

"Shut the fuck up, asshole." Jack leaned forward again and gave me an angry look. "Rachel's a nice girl, but she ain't the fucking Queen of England. You deserve her."

"If she found out what I'd done, where I've been, she'd -"

"You don't know what she'd do. You barely fucking talk to her. Why don't you try getting to know her, you douche? Or, fuck her brains out until she doesn't care what you did in your past."

"Rachel's smart and -"

"You're smart too. Fuck, you read enough goddamn books to fill a fucking library. Just because you've been in prison doesn't mean you can't have the woman you love."

I winced and glanced at the doorway. "Keep your voice down, and I don't love Rachel."

Jack bellowed laughter. "Jesus fucking Christ, you're drowning in that river of denial."

"Shut up."

"If you don't love her, then why are you losing your shit the first time you see another man on her? Why are you telling her that her cherry is yours?"

"Maybe I have a fetish for virgins."

Jack laughed so hard that beer burbled out of his bottle and landed on his jeans. "A virgin fetish?"

I just shrugged. It didn't exactly make me feel like a good guy, but yeah, Rachel being a virgin got my motor going. Knowing that no one else had been in her pussy, that it would only be my cock she'd ever know the feel of, made me harder than a fucking rock.

I'd spent the last three years fantasizing about taking her virgin pussy. The first sign that she might let someone else have it had made me lose my fucking head. I wanted – *needed* – it to be me who took it.

"Look, you know she wants you, and you want her. Take her, for fuck's sake," Jack said.

"It's not that easy. Rachel is…special. She deserves to have someone who can give her everything she wants. Not some fucked-up ex-con."

"She's a grown-ass woman. She can make her own decision about what she wants."

"Can we just drop it?"

"All I'm saying is that if you want to be the one to pop her cherry, you better get your fucking ass in gear. She's not gonna wait around forever for you."

My best friend had a point. I wanted Rachel's virginity, and I needed to take it. I wasn't an idiot. I knew Rachel had a crush on me. I had ignored it despite my desire for her. There was no future for us. But I had fooled myself into thinking she wouldn't give herself to another man and that she would just pine away for me like she was some princess in a damn tower and I was her knight in shining armor.

Fuck. I *was* an idiot.

THIS IS NOT A GOOD IDEA, REN.

It was a fine idea. I parked on the street, locked my car and walked toward the library. I reached into the back pocket of my jeans and touched the smooth sticks. Rachel had left them on my office desk on Friday night after I had...

My cock swelled against my jeans, and I took a quick look around before adjusting myself. Fuck, I couldn't think about Friday night. I had left Jack's place and told myself to go home. Instead, I had driven to the library.

There was only ten minutes until the library closed. If I were lucky, Rachel would be alone, and I could try to explain what happened Friday night.

Or finish what you started.

Bad idea. Very bad idea. I had just barely restrained myself from taking her at the bar. Taking her at the library wasn't any better. Rachel's first time should be in a proper bed with every part of her glorious body naked and ready for my touch. I'd tease her and torment her, make her come a few times until her tight little pussy was dripping wet. I'd give her my cock and show her just how good I could make her -"

"Asher, you're fantastic at this."

My head snapped up. I'd been so deep in my fantasy about taking Rachel's virginity that I'd nearly walked right by the library. Her soft voice had pulled me back to reality in a damn hurry, though. Especially when it was filled with admiration and… dammit, that had better not be lust.

I hurried up the sidewalk toward the library. Rachel was standing on the steps talking to Asher Stokes. Jealousy ate into my stomach, and my hands clenched into fists. Fuck, I needed to calm down. I was a big guy and could hold my own in a fight, but at 6'6" and over two hundred pounds of what was mostly muscle, Asher Stokes would hand my ass to me in less than five minutes.

I took a deep breath and reigned in my jealousy. Asher worked for a welding company here in town and from the looks of it, he was doing his job and repairing the wrought iron railing on the front steps.

"It almost looks brand new." Rachel hadn't noticed me yet, probably because she was thinking about giving her virginity to that asshole Asher.

"Thanks, Rachel."

My skin grew hotter. Asher was a quiet man, probably the quietest man in the entire goddamn town, so how did Rachel know him well enough for them to be on a first-name basis?

"Do you think you'll be finished by tomorrow or…"

I felt the hard bite of satisfaction when Rachel finally noticed me. Her cheeks turned pink, and she quickly backed up the rest of the steps. "Um, excuse me, Asher. I have to, um… excuse me."

With a final glance at me, she yanked open the heavy wooden door to the library and disappeared inside. Asher turned and studied me as I stalked toward him.

"Stay away from her." My voice was hard. The giant standing in front of me could probably crush my skull in one massive hand, but I didn't fucking care. He didn't get to have Rachel.

"What if I don't?" Asher leaned against part of the railing.

Why did I get the feeling he was toying with me? "She belongs to me."

Asher glanced at the door. "Does she know that?"

"Stay away from her, Stokes. This is your last warning."

A grin hovered on his lips. "Relax. I'm not after your woman."

I wanted to believe him, but my jealousy and rage wouldn't quite let me.

Asher gave me a look that suggested he'd stomp me like a bug if I got too close before packing up his tools. I walked up the stairs, yanked open the door, and entered the library.

Despite my love of reading, I'd only been here a handful of times, and only when I was confident that Rachel wasn't working. I hadn't been here at all in the last year. My obsession had reached the point that it didn't matter whether she was working. Just being in the library made me restless and anxious for her.

I looked around as I walked toward the front desk. There wasn't anyone browsing the books, and Rachel was alone at the desk. Her hair was in its usual bun, and she wore an ankle-length skirt and a shirt buttoned to her throat. It was on the looser side, but it didn't matter. I had seen her tits, had touched her nipples, and listened to her moan. The sight of her beautiful breasts in that fire-engine red bra was burned into my damn memory. I stared at her chest, wondering if she was wearing that bra today. I was itching to find out.

Her arms crossed over her chest, and she cleared her throat. I lifted my gaze to her face. Her cheeks were pink, and her lips were wet as though she'd licked them. I could barely hold in my groan when her tongue darted out and licked her bottom lip.

Christ, I wanted to fuck her mouth so bad.

"The library is closed, Mr. Parker."

I checked my watch. "It closes in two minutes."

She scowled at me. "If you want a book, you'll have to come back in the morning. We open at nine."

"I'm not here for a book."

"Then you should leave, Mr. Parker."

"Ren."

"I – what?"

"What happened to calling me Ren?"

"I don't think… that is… I've decided I don't know you well enough to call you Ren."

"Is that so, Rachel?" I leaned over the desk, and she licked her bottom lip again.

"Ms. Banks," she whispered. "You may call me Ms. Banks."

I grinned at her. All my good intentions had scattered to the fucking wind the moment I saw her. The moment I smelled her.

"I've had my fingers in your sweet little pussy, made you come all over them, and I'm not allowed to call you Rachel?"

Her mouth dropped open, and I groaned out loud. The urge to push her to her knees and fill her mouth with my cock was almost too difficult to resist.

"Don't – don't be crude, Mr. Parker."

"You like it when I'm crude."

"No, I don't."

I just grinned at her. "I have something for you, Rachel."

"Wh-what?"

My grin widened when her gaze flickered to my crotch. Fuck, she was just the sweetest little thing. I couldn't wait to be balls-deep inside of her.

"Eyes up here, sweetheart."

Her cheeks turned an alarming shade of red as she whipped her head up. "I wasn't looking at – I mean…what do you want?"

Before I could answer, Asher's low voice came from my left. "You okay, Rachel?"

Rachel stared at Asher. "Yes, of course."

"You need me to stay while you lock up?" Asher's gaze fell on me, and I ignored my urge to cave in his skull. Like I would ever fucking hurt my sweet Rachel.

"Stay?" Rachel gave him a blank look.

"He thinks you're afraid of me," I said.

She blinked in surprise before shaking her head. "No, I'm not afraid of Ren. He's… we're…"

"Friends," I supplied. "Excellent friends."

"We're not friends," she gave me a scathing look, "but I am not afraid of him. Thank you, Asher. I'll see you tomorrow."

She gave him a warm smile, and my jealousy cranked up another notch. I'd never been jealous like this with a woman before, and I had no idea what to do with it. My instinct to sling Rachel over my shoulder and carry her off to my house while beating on my chest seemed… unwise.

"Good night, Rachel."

"Good night, Asher."

The big man turned to leave.

"Good night, Asher," I called after him. He studied me, and I gave him a shit-eating grin that practically screamed, 'Take a swing at me.'

Luckily for me, he just turned and walked away. Christ, I really was trying to get myself a nice extended stay at the fucking hospital.

Rachel followed him to the door and locked it when he left. I considered it a victory that she hadn't kicked me out yet. I studied her curvy body as she returned to the front desk. She took a stack of books from the desk and carried them to one of the carts at the end of an aisle of books. She set them on the cart and grabbed one to shelve it.

I picked up a book and watched as she shelved the one she carried. When she was done, I handed her the book I held.

"Thank you. Uh, what did you have for me?"

I grinned at her, and she turned scarlet as her gaze drifted to my crotch again.

"Sweetheart, when we're in public, you have to stop looking at my cock like you want to suck on it like a lollipop."

"I'm not."

I think she was aiming for indignant, but she just sounded breathless and turned on as fuck.

My grin got wider, and she gave me a furious look. "I am not interested in sucking on your-your penis."

Not only would I teach Rachel how to suck my dick, but I would make it my mission to have her talking filthy while she did it.

"It's called a cock, sweetheart."

"Maybe to someone with a limited vocabulary." She gave me a haughty look that only made my dick harder. "Regardless, I'm not sucking -"

"That's right, I almost forgot. You're not going to suck my dick until I eat your pussy first."

If I had thought her cheeks were red before, now they looked like they would burst into flames. "I – I want no such thing."

"That isn't what you told Madison in the coffee shop."

"It's very rude to listen to private conversations, Mr. Parker."

She made a good point, but I hadn't been purposely eavesdropping. I was passing by her table to catch a hint of her perfume and see the gleam of her dark hair in the sunlight. Hearing her say she would make me eat her pussy had thrown me so far down a rabbit hole of dirty fantasies that I was surprised I hadn't taken her home right then and there and fucked her senseless.

After I ate out her pussy, of course.

"You were talking very loudly," I teased.

She shelved the book with a hard thump. "I wasn't talking about you."

"You were."

A scowl crossed her pretty face. "Can you just leave, please? I don't want to talk to you."

She tried to slide by me, and I cupped her elbow and stopped her. "Since when?" I leaned down and buried my face in her neck, inhaling the scent of her skin. "I know you have a crush on me, Rachel."

"Had, Mr. Parker. I *had* a crush on you." Her voice was low and husky with need.

I straightened and slid my hand around her waist, drawing her up until my erection pressed against her belly. Her soft moan and her almost imperceptible rubbing against it lit me up like a fucking candle.

"What's changed?" I ran my thumb over her lower lip.

"You-you kicked me out of your office Friday night, and you were rude and coarse and…"

Another soft little moan when I traced her collarbone through the thin material of her shirt.

"I also gave you your first orgasm, didn't I?"

"Not my first." She gave me a defiant look. "I might be a virgin, but I'm not a prude. I masturbate as much as the next girl."

I laughed, and she gave me an uncertain look tinged with embarrassment. God, she was so fucking sweet.

"I meant," I kissed the tip of her nose, "that I was the first man to make you come."

"Oh, well, I…maybe you were. But you still…"

"Do you use a vibrator or a dildo, Rachel?"

Her mouth dropped open, and she stared at me. "What?"

"When you masturbate. Do you use a vibrator or a dildo in your virgin pussy?"

"Well … neither."

"Just your fingers, then?"

I could see the answer on her face before she shook her head no.

My cock swelled against my jeans, and I moved my hand down to cup her delightful ass. I kneaded it as I rubbed my dick against her. "So, you've never had anything in your pussy, sweetheart? Do you just rub your sweet clit when you touch yourself?"

"Yes," she whispered.

Fuck. I was a total ass, but it made me even hotter to know that her pussy had never taken a vibrator or even fingers. Of course, that was about to change. Right here and right now.

My hand tightened on her ass, and she made a soft squeak. "It was awful of you to kick me out after making me say those things."

"It was."

My quick agreement made her jerk against my hard body.

"I'm sorry for doing that, sweetheart. It was a dick move, and I won't do it again."

She blinked at me. "I – okay?"

I grinned and leaned down to nuzzle her neck before walking her backward toward the big round table near the wall.

"Of course, an apology isn't enough to compensate for my terrible behaviour, is it?"

"What do you mean?' Her eyes widened when I gripped

her around the waist and lifted her. I sat her on the table, and she immediately closed her legs before I could step between them.

"Don't lift me like that again," she said. "You'll hurt yourself."

I just laughed. "Sweetheart, I can handle your curves."

She crossed her arms over her torso. "What are you doing?"

"Making up for being an asshole to you on Friday night."

"Madison kept telling me you were a nice guy and sweeter than you seemed."

"She's right. I'm very sweet." I plucked at the first button of her shirt.

"Not that sweet. More like -"

I dipped my head and covered her mouth with mine, thrusting my tongue between those soft lips and licking at her tongue. She moaned into my mouth and returned my kiss. Tentatively at first, but with increasing enthusiasm the longer I kissed her. I broke the kiss, allowed her to take some breaths, and dove back in.

Her hands curled around my waist, her fingers digging into my sides. I tugged on her thighs, and when she didn't open them for me, I pulled back.

"Spread your legs, Rachel."

"Ren -"

"Spread them for me right now."

Her legs parted, and I pushed them apart as far as her skirt would allow before stepping between them and pressing my dick against her. I cupped her ass and made her grind her pussy against me. She shuddered all over, and I kissed her again.

When she was pressing her pelvis rhythmically against my cock, I unbuttoned her shirt and pushed it off her shoulders and down her arms. I leaned back and made a low groan. Her bra was a navy blue push-up, and I wanted to bury my face between her glorious tits. I reached behind her, and she gave me a startled look when I unhooked her bra.

"What are you doing?" She crossed her arms over her breasts to keep her bra from sliding off.

"I want to see your gorgeous tits, sweetheart." The flush was rising up her chest, and I tugged on the shoulder straps of her bra, sliding them down her arms. "Move your arms."

She refused, and I leaned down and nipped at her bottom lip. "They belong to me, remember? Show them to me."

"Ren, we can't -"

"Show them to me."

She stared at my mouth and then dropped her arms. I pulled her bra away and dropped it to the floor.

"Sweetheart, I love your tits. Someday I'm going to fuck them."

"What do you mean?"

"It means," I cupped her breasts and pushed them together, "you lie on your back and push your tits together for me, just like this. Then I straddle you and slide my dick back and forth between your beautiful tits."

She bit her bottom lip. "I want to see your cock."

I rubbed my thumbs over her nipples until they were hard little peaks. "Soon, sweetheart."

"Ren, no. I want to see it right now. Before you – oh my goodness!"

I bent my head and took one hard nipple into my mouth. I licked it and sucked it and teased it with my teeth and tongue as her hands threaded through my hair. Her back arched, shoving more of her breast into my mouth. I cupped her other breast, pulling on her nipple as she made little moans and squeaks of pleasure.

182

I straightened and pulled the sticks from the bun in her hair, shoving them into the back pocket of my jeans next to the other sticks. Her hair tumbled to nearly her waist, and I smoothed it back from her face. It was as soft as silk, and I tugged on one lock. "You should wear your hair down more often."

She chewed at her bottom lip. "I – it doesn't look good when it's down."

"It looks beautiful. You're beautiful, sweetheart."

"Thank you. You – you're beautiful too."

I pushed on her shoulders. "Lie back, Rachel."

"W-why?"

"Because I'm going to eat your pussy."

"What? No, you can't!"

"Why not?" I placed one hand between her breasts and applied gentle, steady pressure until she was flat on her back on the table. I leaned over her, preventing her from sitting back up and palmed one heavy breast.

"Because this is where I work." Her pelvis thrust against mine when I pinched her nipple.

"The library is closed."

"I know, but…"

"Are there security cameras in here?" I grinned at her as I rolled her nipple between my finger and thumb.

"I – oh God – um, no. Just outside."

"Then there's no one here to see me eat your sweet pussy." My hands were already reaching for her skirt and I pushed it up her nylon-clad legs. "Hips up, sweetheart."

I waited for her to refuse, and I couldn't stop my grin of satisfaction when she braced her arms on the table and lifted her hips. I quickly pushed her skirt up around her waist before she could change her mind.

"That's my good girl. Now, I'm going to…holy fuck." All

the spit dried up in my mouth as I straightened and looked down at Rachel's pussy.

"What's wrong?" She automatically covered her crotch with her hands. "Oh God, let me up. I can't -"

"Hush, sweetheart." I pulled her hands away and pinned them at her hips. "Let me look at you."

Rachel was wearing a pair of silk, dark blue panties with a matching garter belt and black stockings. My cock was so hard it was threatening to tear a hole through my jeans. Fuck, if I'd known Rachel dressed like this under her long skirts and loose shirts, I wouldn't have been such an idiot and waited so long to make her mine.

"Ren?" Her voice was thick with uncertainty, and her entire body had tensed. "Please let me go."

I released her hands, but when she tried to pull her skirt down, I shook my head. "Don't do that. You're so fucking sexy, Rachel."

Her hands stilled on her skirt. "I am?"

I traced the top of her stockings with my fingers. "Fuck, yes. Do you wear garters and stockings every day?"

"Almost every day. I like to wear pretty, um, underthings."

"They're beautiful." I ran my finger along the waistband of her panties. "I'm going to take these off you now, sweetheart."

I expected her to argue, but she just stared at me with her dark eyes and lifted her hips when I tugged on her panties.

"Good girl," I praised again. I pulled them down her thighs and calves and slipped off her shoes for her before removing her panties entirely and stuffing them in the front pocket of my jeans.

"Feet on the table." I cupped her calves and lifted her legs before she could argue. She planted her feet on the table, and I grinned when I studied her pussy. Her hands covered it completely from my view, and I ran my fingers over the back of her hands. God, I loved how shy and sweet she was.

"Let me see your pretty pussy, sweetheart."

Her hands were trembling. I lifted them and held them tight for a moment as I looked her in the eye. "Relax, Rachel."

"You don't have to do this," she whispered.

I kissed her knuckles. "Sweetheart, I've been dreaming about tasting your sweet pussy for three years."

Her eyes widened. "Seriously?"

"Yeah, sweet one. Rest your hands on the table."

She pressed her hands into the table, making a little nervous squeak when I placed my hands on her inner thighs. "Open your legs nice and wide for me, sweetheart."

I pressed on her smooth thighs, my fingers tugging on her garter straps. She opened her legs, and I pushed them even wider before staring down at her pussy.

"Such a pretty little pussy, Rachel." I touched the small triangle of dark hair at the top of her pussy before running my fingers over her plump and swollen lips. I held my hand up so she could see the moisture on my fingers. "So wet for me."

"Ren, I – oh!"

I had pressed on the bud of her clit that was already protruding from her lips. Her hips jerked, and I pressed my other hand against the curve of her lower belly. "Don't move, sweetheart."

I leaned down, and she made a breathless moan when I licked her pussy lips. I lifted my head and smiled at her. "Sweetest little pussy ever."

"Oh God," she moaned. "Ren, please."

"You want more?"

"Yes." Her hips were already rising. "Yes, do that again."

"Whatever you want, sweetheart."

I liked her lips again before circling her wet hole with my tongue.

"Oh, oh my goodness!" Her low cry made me smile, and I licked my way up to her swollen clit. I flicked it with my tongue and caught her by the hips when she shuddered and nearly slid off the table.

"Careful, sweetheart."

She gave me a pleading look. "Please, oh please."

I bent my head, parted her wet pussy lips with my fingers and licked her clit with a wide, flat stroke of my tongue. She cried out, her pelvis thrusting into my face and her hands grabbing onto my head.

Fuck, her reaction was so hot it was pushing me over the edge. I reached down and unbuttoned and unzipped my jeans. I pulled my dick out and rubbed it roughly as I sucked on Rachel's clit.

She shrieked, the sound echoing through the library, before grinding her pussy against my mouth. I took my hand off my aching dick and pressed my index finger against her virgin hole. I licked and sucked on her clit for a few minutes more. When she was moaning and wiggling wildly, I straightened and stared at her jiggling tits. I rubbed her clit with the pad of my thumb as I slowly slid my finger into her hot, wet entrance.

She froze, her eyes squinting shut and her hands squeezing the table's edge. "Ren? Is that…"

"Just my finger, sweetheart. Relax for me." I circled her clit and then rubbed it firmly. Her pelvis rose, and her pussy swallowed my finger right to the last knuckle.

"Good girl." I slowly eased a second finger into her while I massaged her clit.

"I want to come," she moaned.

"Soon, sweetheart. You're so tight. You feel so good

around my fingers." I made a few experimental thrusts with my fingers, and her pussy squeezed around them. I groaned. My dick was rubbing against her thigh and smearing precum all over her nylons, but I couldn't fucking help it. Rachel was so goddamn hot, and the way she squeezed my fingers was just about enough to make me come all over her.

I hesitated for only a second before burying my face in her pussy again. Fuck it. I would make her come, and then I'd fuck her. I'd waited three fucking years for Rachel's virgin pussy, I couldn't wait any longer.

I licked and sucked on her clit until she made another loud shriek, and her entire body arched off the table. She came all over my face, her body shuddering and her thighs squeezing around my head. I pushed her thighs apart and licked away her sweet cream as she moaned and shook. Her pussy was clenching and unclenching around my fingers. I pulled my fingers free, and she made a cry of disappointment.

"I know, sweetheart," I said. "Your little pussy needs to be filled, doesn't it?"

"Yes," she whimpered.

"Do you want my cock?" I held my dick in my hand and stroked it roughly.

Her eyelids fluttered open, and I watched as she stared at my dick. She nodded, although I could see the anxiety on her face, and I squeezed one thigh. "I'll go slow, sweetheart. But I can't wait any longer. I need to fuck you."

I rubbed the head of my dick along her soaking wet slit. She shivered all over and jerked away when I rubbed her clit.

"Too sensitive?" I kneaded her thigh.

"A-a little," she gasped out.

I moved my cock down to her entrance. I pushed, and she moaned in response. I pushed the head of my cock into her and stopped. Fuck, she was so goddamn tight. I needed to do some deep breathing exercises, or I'd shove my entire dick into her pussy without a second thought.

"Ren? Why are you stopping?"

"Give me a minute, sweetheart. I want to go slow, but I -"

The pounding on the library's front door made us jerk wildly. Another inch slid into her tight pussy, and Rachel made a strangled sound that had too much pain in it. I pulled out of her in a hurry, sat her up, and cupped her face. "Sweetheart, I'm sorry. Are you okay?"

"I, yeah, I'm okay. I just -"

"Rachel! Rachel, open up! Are you in there? Open the door!"

The woman's voice was muffled, but I could hear the anger in it.

"Who the fuck is that?" I said as Rachel scrambled off the table and shoved her skirt down.

She reached for her bra, giving me a look of shame. "My mother."

CHAPTER 3

Rachel

I wanted to die.

I wanted to drop dead right there in the library. I had been seconds away from finally losing my virginity to Ren Parker, and my *mother* was interrupting us like I was a stupid teenage girl.

Could a person die of shame? They could, right?

I whipped around until my back was to Ren and threw my bra on. I raked the straps up my arms. "Can you do me up?"

Ren fumbled at the hooks as my mother's muffled but clearly understandable voice screeched through the door. "Rachel! I know you're in there. Open the door. Why are you ignoring me? I've been waiting fifteen minutes for you!"

"Hurry!" I muttered.

"Sorry, sweetheart, I'm better at unhooking these." His voice held more than a hint of laughter in it.

"This is not funny."

"It's kind of funny." He finished doing up my bra and I grabbed my shirt as my mother pounded on the door again.

This time, I could hear the panic in her voice. "Rachel? This isn't funny, young lady! I'm about thirty seconds away from calling the police. Do you hear me?"

"Fuck!" I yanked my shirt on and buttoned it as Ren tucked away his penis and buttoned his jeans.

"What's she doing here?" he asked.

"Her car is in the shop, so she borrowed mine and said she would pick me up after work. I completely forgot."

I pushed my feet into my shoes and hurried toward the front door, straightening my shirt and skirt compulsively as Ren followed me. I was trying to think of an excuse for why Ren was in the library with me, but I was barely thinking straight. Ren had just eaten my pussy until I had the best orgasm of my life. Ren had almost fucked me. Would be fucking me if it hadn't been for my...

Oh shit.

I stopped with my hand on the lock and gave Ren a frantic look. "My panties. Where are they?"

I kept my voice pitched low, but my mother had the hearing of a hawk. She immediately pounded on the door again. "Rachel? Is that you? Open the door right this minute!"

Ren winked at me and pulled a bit of my panties out of his pocket. "I've got them right here."

"Give them to me." I held out my hand, glaring at him when he shoved them back into his pocket.

"No time, sweetheart."

"Ren, I need -"

"Rachel! Open the door!"

Groaning inwardly, I smoothed my hair and reached for the door. "Don't say a word."

"Yes, ma'am."

Why did he have to be so friggin' sexy?

I unlocked the door and pulled it open, blocking the doorway with my chubby body. My mother glared at me. "What are you doing?"

"Just closing up, Mom. I'm running a little late, but I won't be much longer. Give me five minutes, and I'll meet you in the car."

"I'll wait for you in here." She shoved past me and looked me up and down. "You look awful today. How often have I told you not to wear your hair down, Rachel? It makes your face look even fatter, and your -"

"I think she looks beautiful."

My mother screeched and swung around to stare at Ren. "Who – what are you doing here?"

"Mom, this is Ren Parker. He owns Ren's Bar. He's looking for a book."

Please don't insult him. Please don't insult him.

"Since when do bartenders read?"

"Mom! Stop it."

"What? Bartenders don't read, Rachel."

"How many bartenders do you know, Mrs. Banks?" Ren's voice was polite, but I could see the anger brewing on his face.

"None." She sniffed. "We don't associate with your type of people."

"Enough, Mom." I took my mother's arm and tugged her away. "You're being rude."

"Who cares? He's below us and -"

"Stop it." I shook her roughly, and she yanked her arm from my grip.

"What is going on with you? Are you forgetting all that I've sacrificed for you?"

"No," I said in a low voice. "But Ren is – is a customer at the library, and I'm not letting you insult him. Do you want me to lose my job? Is that it?"

"You concentrate way too much on your job. You don't have the looks to catch a man, so you need to work on your personality. If you spent less time working extra shifts at the library and more time working on your social skills, you might not be single and alone. You need -"

I walked away before she could finish her sentence. I had no desire for Ren to hear all about my boring personality and awkward social behaviour. I stopped in front of Ren and gave him a please-get-the-hell-out-of-here look. "Mr. Parker, if you give me a few days, I'll see if I can find that book you're looking for at one of the other libraries and have it transferred."

Ren studied me for a moment before nodding. "Sure. Thank you, Rachel."

"You're welcome."

He leaned forward, and for one pulse-pounding moment, I thought he would kiss me right there in front of my mother. Instead, he removed an invisible piece of lint from my shirt sleeve and gave me a boyish grin. "Bye."

He turned and opened the library door. Before he could step outside, my mother's voice rang out.

"What is that in your pocket?"

My heart stopped. Just gave up for an entire three seconds before clanging back to life in my chest. I wheezed in a breath as I tried to think of a plausible explanation for why Ren had my panties in his pocket.

"Why do you have those in your back pocket?" My mother demanded.

Ren pulled the two sets of sticks from his pocket and

studied them before holding them out to me. "Right, I almost forgot to give these to you."

My hand was shaking so badly that I almost dropped them. Ren curled his hand around mine, keeping the sticks in my palm. "You okay, sweetheart?"

"Sweetheart?" My mother's voice was high enough to make dogs howl.

I pulled my hand away from Ren's and stepped back. "Yes, Mr. Parker, thank you. Have a good evening."

Hurt flickered across his face, but he smoothed it out, nodded, and left the library. I closed and locked the door behind him before staring at the sticks in my hand. Why were Ren's feelings hurt? And why did it bother me that I hurt his feelings?

"Rachel, what is going on with you and that man?"

"Nothing."

"Don't lie to me. He called you 'sweetheart' and had your hair sticks in his pocket."

I pushed past her and headed toward the front desk. "He's just a flirt, and I dropped the sticks at his bar the other night. He was being nice and was returning them to me."

"Why were you even at the bar? Nice girls don't go to the bar. Were you with Madison again? You know how I feel about that girl. She's a total slut, and if you aren't careful, she's going to drag you down with her. Why, just the other day, Eleanor Rochen told me that she thinks Jacob is sleeping with Madison. Can you believe that? He's twice her age and was her father's best friend. What kind of man sleeps with a child?"

"Madison isn't a child, and Jacob isn't twice her age. He's a nice man," I said.

"He's a sicko. I don't want you hanging out with Madison anymore if she's going to be sleeping with a sick man like that. Oh, and did you hear that Lydia Davis is returning to town? Our idiot mayor is giving her the key to the town. And for what? Because she won some acting award?"

"She won an Emmy, Mom. It's a big deal."

"Well, call me when she wins an Oscar." My mother sniffed. "She was always so stuck up. Her sister isn't much better, you know. I swear, she deliberately gives me the wrong coffee every time I stop at Mugs. I ran into Michelle at the gym the other day, and she said…"

As my mother droned on about the people in our small town, I smiled, nodded, and pretended to listen while I closed my computer. I hated listening to my mother's mean-spirited and petty gossip about the town, but at least she wasn't asking me any more questions about what Ren was doing with me in the library.

"WAIT," MADISON TUCKED HER LEGS UNDER HER AND SETTLED back on the couch, "so, did you and Ren have sex last night in the library or not?"

"I don't know," I admitted.

"How can you not know," Madison said with a grin. "Either he put his dick in you, or he didn't."

"I told you, he started to, but we were interrupted."

"How much did you get?" Madison took a sip of wine.

"What?"

"How much of his dick did you get? If you got the whole thing even just once, your cherry's been officially popped, and I'm opening up a second bottle of wine."

"Uh, I don't think it was the whole thing," I said. "I mean, I know he put the, uh, head in, but I think that's all he got in."

"If it was just the tip, it doesn't count," Madison said as Jacob strolled into the living room.

"Just the tip of what?" He leaned down and pressed a kiss against her mouth.

I turned a truly hellish shade of red as Jacob nodded to me. "Hey, Rachel."

"Hi."

He studied my red cheeks before turning back to Madison. "What are you two talking about?"

"Girl stuff."

"Okay. Well, I'll shower quickly, and then I'll start the steaks."

"Thanks, honey."

He left, and I said, "So, are you two officially living together now?"

"He's basically living here but hasn't sold his place and moved his stuff in yet."

"Is he going to?"

She nodded. "If he knows what's good for him, he will."

I laughed. "I'm happy for you, Mads. You know that, right?"

"Thanks, sweetie. But don't change the subject. I'm making my ruling, and," she pounded out a drum beat on the arm of the couch, "congratulations, Rachel Banks, you are still a virgin."

"Thanks." I drained my glass of wine and jumped up to pour another from the bottle on the coffee table. "Did I mention it hurt a little? Maybe he did pop it and -"

"Were you bleeding after?"

"No, but I did a lot of horseback riding as a teen. My actual hymen is probably long gone."

"Good point. Well, unless Ren was in balls-deep, I still don't think it counts."

My cheeks were still boiling, and Madison grinned at me. "It's adorable how talking about sex makes you blush. Once Ren takes your virginity, I'm going to miss how flustered you get when we talk sex."

I drank more wine. "He's not going to take my virginity. Not after my mother interrupted us. God, it was so humiliating, Mads. One, to be interrupted like I'm some damn teenager, and two, she was so rude to him. She said mean things and -"

"Your mom is a bitch." Madison poured herself more wine. "Scratch that, she's not a bitch. She's a full-on Disney villain. She's Cruella da Ville...no, she's Ursula from The Little Mermaid. If she were a character in a book, she'd be Hannibal Lecter. Minus the cannibalism."

She paused and gave me a suspicious look. "Minus the cannibalism, right, Rach?"

"I dunno. Does eating my self-esteem for breakfast every morning from when I was eleven until I moved out at nineteen count as cannibalism?"

Madison scowled. "All jokes aside, I hate what that woman has done to you."

"She's still my mother."

"Only by blood. I have never met a less mom-like woman in my life, and I grew up without a mother. You need to cut off contact with her, Rach. She's bad for you."

I sighed and stared into my wine glass. I'd had this conversation off and on for years with Madison. She wasn't wrong, my mother was toxic, but she was still my mother. She sometimes said hurtful things only because she wanted what was best for me.

Does she, though? Because it comes off a lot like hatred.

The red in my cheeks faded, and the wine sloshed in my

belly until I felt nauseous. My mother didn't hate me. Mothers didn't hate their children.

"Rachel? You okay?"

"Yes. Just a little too much wine and not enough food."

Madison stood and took my hand. "Come into the kitchen. We'll munch on the veggies while we wait for my man to cook us some meat."

I smiled and squeezed her hand. "Thank you, Mads. I love you. You know that, right?"

"I do," she said. "But, really – who doesn't love me?"

CHAPTER 4

Rachel

Mugs Coffee was one of two coffee shops in our small town. It's prime location on Main Street meant it was always the busier of the two, and this morning was no exception. I joined the line-up, surfing Facebook on my phone as the line slowly shuffled forward. I hadn't slept well last night or Monday night, and I was tired and feeling a little emotional.

I had blown it with Ren. I'd had my chance to lose my virginity to him, and I'd ruined it. He hadn't tried to contact me since Monday night, and I wasn't surprised. Depressed? Hell, yeah. Surprised? Not in the least.

I rubbed my forehead before stuffing my phone into my pocket. The tap on my shoulder made me jump, and I turned. I stared at the vast chest, the blue fabric of his t-shirt stretched to the limit across it, and craned my neck to stare into his face.

"Hello, Rachel."

"Morning, Asher." I smiled at the big man. "You should have told me you liked coffee. I would have picked yours up and brought it to the library."

"Appreciate that, but I usually stop in every morning for coffee."

"You, me, and the rest of the town. So, is today your last day at the library? Our library assistant mentioned yesterday that you said you'd be finishing up today."

He nodded. "Should be done by noon."

"That's good." There was an awkward silence. I'd lived in this town all my life, but I don't think I'd ever spoken to Asher until he was hired to fix the railing at the library. He was a few years older than me, and we had only one year of high school together before he graduated. His sister Isabelle was my age, but she'd been a cheerleader in high school and one of the popular girls, and our paths rarely crossed. She'd moved with their parents to Florida just after graduation.

"Uh, so how is Isabelle doing in Florida?" I asked.

"She's good. Moving back next week."

"Really?"

He nodded but didn't provide any further details.

"Well, that's nice. Is she going to stay with you for a bit or…?"

"For a bit."

"Good, that's good." I tried to think of something else to say and came up with nothing. I really had nothing in common with him. Well, other than the fact that we both went to Ren's Bar. I'd seen him a few times at the bar with Knox Jameson. Knox was a landscaper in town, and he and Asher had been best friends for years.

They were an unlikely pair. Knox was funny and outgoing and never seemed to stop talking. Asher was the quietest man in town. Even my mother couldn't find anything to gossip about when it came to him.

"Your turn."

I stared blankly at Asher. "What?"

"It's your turn." He pointed behind me, and I turned around to see Luna Davis, sister to Lydia, the Emmy-winning and soon-to-be recipient of the key to our fair town, giving me an impatient look.

I stepped up to the counter. "Sorry, Luna. I'll take a venti mocha. Hold the whip. Plus, whatever Asher's having."

Luna's fingers paused on the cash register before she added a venti dark roast to the order.

"You don't have to do that." Asher had joined me at the counter.

"I know. I want to." I watched as Luna's face turned red, and she gave Asher a quick, jittery smile.

"Hi, Asher. How, uh, how are you this morning?"

"Morning." He gave her a brief look before nodding to me. "Thanks for the coffee, Rachel. I appreciate it."

"You're welcome." Shit, compared to how he was with Luna, he was downright chatty with me.

Asher moved to the counter's far end, and I quickly paid for the coffee. "Thanks, Luna."

"You bet." She furtively glanced at Asher as I walked away to join him.

Maybe it was because I had lost my chance at the guy I wanted, or maybe I just wanted someone to get laid, but I decided to try to help her out. "Luna's cute, huh?"

Asher stared down at me, and I cleared my throat. "She's cute, and she's a total sweetheart."

"Didn't know you two were friends."

"We're not. I mean, we're friendly, but we don't, like, hang out together."

"Then how do you know she's a sweetheart?"

Now, it was my turn to go red as Asher arched one thick brow. "Well, I...I mean, I've heard that she's lovely. Not like her sister."

He picked up his coffee from the counter and nodded to me. "See you at the library."

"Okay, bye."

He walked away, and I snuck a quick look at Luna. Despite the long line of customers, she was staring at Asher's ass as he walked out of the coffee shop. She realized I was staring at her and, blushing furiously, turned back to the customer in line.

I WAS MAKING A MISTAKE. NO, I WAS BEING A HOPELESS IDIOT.

After work, I'd gone home and ate dinner before staring blankly at the TV. Half an hour later, I was rummaging through my closet for shirts and jeans that I had deemed too tight. Half an hour after that, I was in my car driving to Ren's Bar.

I pulled open the door and walked into the bar. It was packed full of people, and I groaned inwardly. Shit, I forgot that Wednesday was karaoke night. I studied the tables closest to me. All of them were full, and I didn't want to sit right at the bar. I had come here because I was hoping that Ren still wanted me. But I had lost my nerve, and now all I wanted to do was go back home, take off my stupidly tight shirt and jeans, and crawl into bed.

I turned and ran straight into a hard wall of flesh. A big hand wrapped around my arm and steadied me.

"You okay?"

"Yeah. Thanks, Asher." I smiled at the welder. "You can't seem to get away from me lately, can you?"

He just shrugged. His gaze landed briefly on my tits before he stared at my face again. "You here for the karaoke?"

"God, no. I can't sing. I was just, uh, I thought I would have a drink, but all the tables are full, so… I'm just going to go."

"You can sit with us." Asher took my arm and led me through the crowded bar. Thanks to his size, people naturally moved out of his way, and it took less than a minute for us to get to his table. Knox Jameson was sitting at the table and grinned at me as Asher pulled out a chair so I could sit down.

I sank into it as Knox leaned forward. "Hey there. I'm Knox. You're the librarian, right?"

"Yes. I'm Rachel."

"Nice to meet you, Rachel." He held out his hand, and I shook it. Unlike Asher, his gaze lingered on my breasts, and I self-consciously crossed my arms over my chest. Ren wouldn't like other men staring at them. They belonged to him and –

Shit, what was wrong with me? I abruptly dropped my arms. My boobs didn't belong to Ren. Telling him that in the heat of passion was one thing, but just to start believing it … I was going crazy. I had to be, right?

"Can I get you guys another round or… Rach?"

I smiled at my best friend. "Hi, Mads. How are you?"

She leaned down, the apron around her waist jingling with change, and kissed my cheek. "Hi, sweetie. I'm good. What are you doing here tonight?"

I shrugged. "Just thought I would stop in and say hi to you."

"Isn't that sweet." She pressed her mouth against my ear.

"Ren is here, but in his office. Want me to take you back there?"

"No," I said a little too quickly. "No, I just stopped in for a drink and to say hi to you."

"Oh." She straightened and studied my body. "Your tits look great tonight."

"Madison!" I gave Asher and Knox an embarrassed look.

Knox finished the last of his beer before grinning at me. "She's not wrong."

Madison laughed and grabbed his and Asher's empty beer bottles. "You guys want another?"

"Sure do, gorgeous. What are you doing after work?" Knox gave her a sexy smile.

"Going home to my man," Madison said with a grin. "I'll bring you a glass of wine, Rach."

She walked away, and I tugged self-consciously at my shirt as Knox turned his attention to me. "Guess I'll just have to set my sights on a sweet little bookworm."

"Knock it off," Asher grunted to him.

Knox ignored him. "What do you like to do for fun, Rachel?"

A loud cheer from the audience drowned out my answer. I glanced toward the small dance floor where the karaoke was set up. Luna Davis was picking up the microphone, and she blushed as the crowd cheered again.

"Is she good?" I asked Knox.

He nodded as Madison returned with two more beers and a glass of wine. Before I could reach for my wallet, Asher handed her some bills. "Her glass is on me."

"Thanks, Asher." I took a sip of wine as Madison glanced over at Luna.

"Oh good, Luna's going to sing. She's fucking amazing.

Hell, I think half the people here show up every Wednesday night just to hear her."

She suddenly scowled and waved to someone in the crowd before muttering, "Yeah, yeah. I know you're waiting for your beer, Henry. Keep your damn pants on. I gotta go, Rach."

"Bye, Mads."

She left, and Knox leaned forward. "What are you going to sing, Rachel?"

I laughed. "Nothing. I'd clear the place out as soon as I…"

My voice died as the music started, and Luna began to sing. I stared wide-eyed at the petite redhead before turning to Knox. "Holy shit. She's so good."

"She is." Knox took another swig of beer.

"She could be a professional. Don't you think, Asher?" I turned to the welder when he didn't reply. He stared at Luna, his big hand gripping his beer bottle and his body ramrod straight.

"Asher?"

He jerked and turned toward me. The lust in his gaze took my damn breath away. He made a short nod before immediately turning back to Luna. It was like he couldn't look away, and honestly, I could understand why. Her singing voice was powerful and velvety-smooth, and I had no idea that a voice that big could come out of a woman that small.

I stared at Asher again as Luna's voice floated across the dead-silent bar. It was more than apparent that he wanted her, and I wondered why he had been so cold to her in the coffee shop this morning.

Luna finished her song, and there was a moment of silence before the crowd erupted in loud cheers, whistles, and catcalls.

Luna blushed and said a soft 'thank you' into the microphone before returning to her table. I winced when she tripped over her feet and did a face plant into the floor. Asher jumped to his feet and took a few steps forward, but Madison and the other bartender, Peter, had already helped Luna to her feet. I could see blood trickling from her bottom lip, and she shook her head when Madison said something to her. She pulled a tissue from her pocket and pressed it against her mouth before patting Madison's arm and returning to her chair.

I took another sip of wine as Asher sat back down and drank half of his beer in three big swallows. I had no idea why Asher wasn't going after Luna when it was so obvious he wanted her, but who was I to judge? I wanted Ren, but here I sat, too chicken to go to his office and talk to him. I took another drink of wine. God, I was an idiot.

CHAPTER 5

Ren

"Hey, Ren?"

I glanced up from my computer. "What's up, Madison?"

"I'm going to be taking my break soon, and Peter wanted to know if you can cover the bar when he takes his break. It's slammin' busy tonight, and he doesn't want to leave Mike alone."

"Wednesdays always are. Tell Pete I'll be out in five."

"Okay."

She lingered in my office doorway, and I raised my eyebrows. "What?"

"Nothing." A cheeky grin crossed her face. "Just thought you might want to know that Rachel's here and sitting with Asher Stokes and Knox Jameson."

She closed my door, but I was already on my feet and

crossing the small office. What the hell was Rachel doing here? It was a goddamn Wednesday.

I yanked open my office door and stormed down the hallway and into the bar. It was crowded with people, which normally made me happy, but tonight? Tonight I was pissed that I couldn't find Rachel in the crowd. I started searching the tables one by one as the sound of a dying goose came to my left. I studied the dance floor, grimacing at the blonde woman standing beside the karaoke machine and murdering an Adele song.

I turned back to the tables, my eyes narrowing when I saw Rachel leave her table and head toward the bathrooms. She was wearing tight jeans and a shirt that... shit, it was so tight I could see the outline of the lace on her bra beneath it. My nostrils flared. I don't know what the hell was going on with my sweet Rachel, but her new habit of wearing clothing that showed off her magnificent tits would be the goddamn death of me.

She disappeared into the bathroom, and I waited a few minutes, trying to cool my lust and my jealousy. When I thought I had it under control, I turned my attention to the two men sitting at her table. Anger immediately swallowed me whole, and I made my way to their table, my hands already in fists and my muscles vibrating with rage.

"What the fuck do you think you're doing, asshole?"

Knox nearly spit out his beer as Asher gave me a cool look. "Nice to see you again, Ren."

I leaned down until my face was only inches from his. "I told you to stay away from her. She belongs to me."

"And I told you I wasn't after your woman. Now get your face out of mine."

I refused to move as Knox said, "Ren, you idiot. Walk away before Ash turns you to mincemeat."

"If you go anywhere near her, I'll -"

"Walk. Away." Asher's voice was calm, but I could hear the anger simmering beneath it. It amped me up, and I was getting ready to do something truly stupid when I heard Rachel's soft voice.

"Ren? What are you doing?"

I straightened and held out my hand. "Come with me."

To my relief, she didn't argue, just took my hand in her small one. I walked her across the bar and out the door.

"Ren? Where are we going?"

I didn't reply as I searched the parking lot for her car. When I found it, I walked briskly toward it as Rachel hurried beside me.

When I stopped beside her car, she pulled her hand from mine and gave me a confused look. "What are you doing?"

"Get in your car and go home, Rachel."

She glared at me. "No."

"Yes."

"You're not my damn boss, Ren Parker. I'm going back to Asher and Knox and -"

I pulled her into my arms, my hand cupping the back of her neck as I scowled down at her. "You stay away from the both of them. You belong to me, and I don't want you anywhere near that manwhore Knox Jameson."

"I don't belong to you. I'm a person, not a -"

Hearing her say she didn't belong to me sent jealousy rocketing through my body. I kissed her, stopping her protests. She returned my kiss and didn't object when I shoved my tongue deep into her mouth.

I kissed her until I was desperate for oxygen. I pulled away, both of us gasping for air, as she stared wide-eyed at me.

I cupped her face and rubbed my thumb along her bottom lip. "You belong to me. Say it."

"I belong to you," she whispered.

"That's right. Now, get in your car and go home."

"I don't want to. We need to talk about -"

I squeezed her ass and nipped her bottom lip. "Go home, strip down to your panties and wait for me in your bedroom."

"I – what?"

"Go home, take off everything but your panties and wait for me in your bedroom. I'll be there in an hour. I want you to lie on your bed and think about how good it will feel when I fuck you, Rachel."

"Ren," she moaned as I squeezed her ass again and then nuzzled her neck.

"Go home, Rachel. Go home and think about me kissing you, touching you, fucking you. I want you wet when I get there, but don't touch your sweet pussy. That's for my fingers only. Do you understand?"

"Yes."

"Good." I touched her hair piled on her head in its usual bun. "I want your hair down when I get there."

"O-okay."

I kissed her once more, palming her ass through her jeans and pressing my erection against her so she could see what she fucking did to me. "Be careful driving home."

"I will."

"That's my good girl. I'll see you in an hour."

RACHEL'S HOUSE WAS SMALL AND COZY. SHE HAD LEFT THE front door unlocked for me, and despite never being in her house before, it took me less than a minute to find her bedroom. I eased open the door, and my dick immediately hardened. Rachel looked like a goddess in the dim glow of the lamp next to the bed. She was wearing just a pair of pink panties and lying on the bed, staring at the ceiling. I sat down on the bed beside her and studied her gorgeous body. Her nipples were hard points, and her breathing was short and shallow. She continued to stare at the ceiling, but I could see the nervousness etched into her face.

"Sweetheart -"

"I don't have any condoms. I thought I did, but they're expired because I was waiting for…"

Her cheeks turned pink. She still wouldn't look at me, and she made a nervous gasp when I rested my hand on her abdomen.

"Look at me, sweetheart."

She pressed her lips together before turning her head. Her dark eyes were wide with anxiety, and I rubbed her warm skin. "Waiting for what, Rachel?"

She took a deep breath. "You. I wanted you to be my first."

A smug grin crossed my face. I knew it made me look like a total dickhead, but I couldn't help it.

The flush on her cheeks moved down her throat and over her chest. "Stop looking so smug."

I stripped off my t-shirt and relaxed on my side next to her. I traced tiny circles between her breasts as she made a low moan. "Did you do what I asked, sweetheart? Did you think about me fucking you? Are you wet for me now?"

Her gaze skittered away from mine. "I wanted to. I mean, I tried to, but I got anxious about the condom thing, and I didn't know if I should text you, but then I didn't have your number anyway. And I was afraid if I told you I didn't have condoms, you wouldn't come over, and I really wanted you to come over. But I'm an idiot because it's not like we're going to have sex without a condom, and now I've messed everything up again, and I'm going to be a virgin for the rest of my fucking life!"

She dragged in a breath, and before she could say anything else, I leaned over and kissed her. I pushed my tongue into her mouth, flicking at hers as I threaded my fingers into her long, soft hair. When I pulled back, she was breathless, and the anxiety had disappeared from her gaze.

"Better?" I petted her long hair and pressed a kiss against her forehead.

"Yes."

"Good." I traced her collarbone with the tips of my fingers. "I have condoms, sweetheart."

"Oh, thank God."

The relief in her voice made me smile. I took her hand and linked my fingers with hers. "Are you on the pill, Rachel?"

"Yeah. My period is pretty bad if I'm not, so I… uh, sorry, that's not something you want to know."

She was wrong. I wanted to know everything about her.

She bit her lip. "Anyway, I am, but if you have condoms, what does it matter?"

I let go of her hand and reached into my back pocket for my phone. She watched with confusion as I tapped something into my phone before turning the screen toward her. "Look at this."

She studied the screen, her forehead wrinkling in a genuinely adorable way. "Is that – are these your medical records?"

I nodded, and she gave me another look of confusion. "Why do you have these in your phone?"

"Because I want to fuck you without a condom, sweetheart. I want nothing between us for your first time. I want to feel the warmth and wetness of your pussy around my bare cock, so I want you to see that I'm infection free. But, if you're still not comfortable with that, then I'll use a condom."

She stared at me for a moment before plucking my phone from my grip. She scrolled across the screen, reading my records with the careful concentration of a lawyer reviewing a contract. I couldn't stop my grin, and she flushed a little when she finally returned my phone.

"What?"

"Nothing. I just love how carefully you read it."

"It's important to know your boyfriend's past sexual history. A girl has to protect her body from...oh God, I didn't mean boyfriend. I meant a random guy that you have sex with. Wait... not that you're just a random guy. You're, um -"

I kissed her again and could almost feel her relief at how I'd stopped the flow of words. She returned my kisses eagerly, and I cupped her bare breast, loving the softness of her skin. I flicked her nipple with my thumb, and she gasped into my mouth before arching her back.

I pulled back, and she pouted at me. "Please, Ren."

"Soon. We haven't finished our conversation. Will you let me take you bare, sweetheart?"

"Yes." There was no hesitation in her voice, and the last of my well-hidden anxiety disappeared.

"I'm gonna make you feel so good, Rach," I whispered into her ear as I cupped her breast again. I sucked on her earlobe. "Let's get naked. What do you say?"

Her soft laugh turned into a moan when I pulled on her hard nipple. "Yes. Yes, naked is an excellent idea."

CHAPTER 6

Rachel

I watched with barely concealed eagerness as Ren sat up on the side of the bed. The muscles in his back flexed as he took off his socks, and I wanted to touch his warm, hard skin.

So, touch him then.

I sat up and ran my fingers down his spine. He made a low groan, and I moved to my knees behind him and pressed my breasts against his back before kissing his shoulder. I licked my way to his neck and nipped his rough skin as I slid my arms around him and rubbed his flat abdomen.

I sucked on his earlobe and ran my hands up to his broad chest, touching the coarse hair that covered it. My long hair was everywhere, brushing against his body and getting in my face. I reached for the hair elastic on my nightstand, but Ren took my hand and shook his head.

"No. Keep your hair down for me."

He reached up and took a lock of my hair, rubbing it through his fingers. "It's so soft, so beautiful."

"Thank you," I whispered. I ran my right hand down toward the waistband of his jeans, but when I tried to cup his dick through the denim, he caught my hand again and pulled it away.

"I'm sorry." Dull embarrassment coated my apology.

"Don't be sorry. If you touch me, I'm going to explode all over your hand."

I giggled a bit nervously, and he squeezed my hand before standing. He turned and shook his head when I went to cover my naked breasts. "No, sweetheart. Don't be shy. You're beautiful."

I lowered my arms and watched the need in his eyes flare. It made my nipples harden into painful buds and my pussy wet. I squeezed my legs together, for once not thinking about the chunkiness of my thighs. The way Ren looked at me, the prominent bulge of his erection against his jeans, made me feel as beautiful as he said I was.

He was undoing his jeans, and I watched with a mixture of anticipation and trepidation as he pushed them and his briefs down his muscular thighs. His cock popped free, and my anxiety kicked it up a notch. It looked huge to me, huge and almost angry, with its head a dark red and a bead of precum at the tip.

He smiled at me as he removed his clothing. "Nervous?"

"A little. I'm worried it's going to hurt, and I'm not great with pain. I did a lot of horseback riding as a teenager, so I'm pretty sure that I don't, like, have a hymen left or anything, so I doubt I'll bleed, but I'm still…"

Rachel. Stop talking. Please.

"Oh God, sorry." I gave him an embarrassed look.

"For what?"

"I'm babbling."

"I don't mind." He stepped closer and stroked my hair. "I'll take my time, sweetheart."

"Will you?"

He nodded. "I've waited three years. I can wait a little longer."

My jaw dropped as he moved closer. We were the same height, with me on my knees on the bed and him standing. His hard chest pressed against my breasts, and I could feel his dick brushing against my lower belly. He gathered my hair in his hands and smoothed it down my back.

"Three years," I whispered. "You've wanted me for three years?"

"Yes."

"Why?"

He slid one arm around my waist and pulled me up tight against him. "Why? Because you're beautiful, because you're sexy, because you were meant for me."

"Why did you wait so long? You knew I had a crush on you."

He cupped my breast and ran his thumb over my nipple. "Enough questions for now, sweetheart."

He kissed me and cupped and kneaded my breasts until hard beats of lust pulsed through my body. I rubbed against him, made soft mewing noises into his mouth, and clutched at his waist as I forgot my nervousness. God, I wanted him so much.

When his hand slid into my panties, I spread my legs eagerly, ready for the pleasure he would give me. He didn't disappoint. His rough fingers parted my swollen pussy lips and rubbed against my clit. He dipped his head and sucked on my nipple as I arched my back and begged for more.

I was already on the edge, and to my relief, he didn't tease. Instead, he rubbed my clit with firm and steady pressure as he sucked and licked my nipples. I writhed against him, my fingers digging into his broad back as he brought me to the edge of my climax and pushed me over with a hard tug of my clit. I moaned and shook against him, the pleasure flooding through my entire body as Ren pushed two fingers deep into my pussy. I squeezed around him, and he groaned before kissing me hard again.

"I need to fuck you," he whispered against my mouth.

"Yes," I said. "Please, Ren. I've waited so long."

He pulled his fingers out of my pussy and pushed my panties down to my knees. "On your back, sweetheart."

I moved to my back, and Ren pulled my panties off my legs and dropped them on the floor. He knelt in front of me and pushed on my knees. "Open for me."

The pleasure of my orgasm was fading, and my anxiety was returning. What if it hurt? I wasn't lying when I told Ren I wasn't great with pain. It was embarrassing, but I'd always been a total wimp. What if I started crying? Worse, what if I screamed or told him to stop and he didn't, or he got angry and -"

"Sweetheart."

Ren's low voice broke through my frantic inner babbling, and I stared at him as he rubbed the outside of my thighs. "Trust me."

I studied him for a moment longer before spreading my thighs wide. I trusted Ren and that he would do everything he could to make it good for me.

He stroked my inner thighs before leaning down and kissing me. His cock rubbed against my pussy, but I didn't feel any anxiety, just a powerful desire for him. He reached between us and rubbed my pussy before showing me the moisture on his fingers.

"Look how wet you are for me," he said in a low voice. "You're ready for me, sweetheart."

"Yes," I whispered as he propped himself above me on one hand and used the other to guide his cock to my entrance. He pressed the head against me before resting his other hand next to my head.

I closed my eyes as he pushed the head of his cock into me. He stopped and brushed a kiss against my mouth.

"Rachel." His voice was hoarse, on the edge of his control. "Open your eyes, sweetheart."

I did what he asked and stared up at him.

"That's my good girl. I want you to look at me while I make you mine. Can you do that?"

"Yes, Ren." I clutched at his narrow waist and stared into his eyes as he pushed steadily into my body. The cords in his neck stood out, and I could see a vein throbbing at his temple, but he kept the same slow pace. To my surprise there was no pain, just an uncomfortable feeling of fullness. Even that seemed to dissipate as he pushed deeper, and my inner walls stretched around his invading cock.

"Good, sweetheart?" He groaned.

"Yes," I whispered, "don't stop."

He made another low groan and pushed until his pelvis was pressing against mine. I was completely impaled on his thick cock, and he raised a shaking hand and cupped my face for a moment. "Now, you really do belong to me."

"I belong to you," I whispered. I meant it. Every part of me screamed that I was Ren's and always would be.

He leaned down and rested his forehead against mine, his

warm breath washing over me. "I have to move. Are you okay?"

"Yes. It feels good."

I'd barely gotten the words out before Ren was moving in and out of me with long, deep strokes. I stared up at him and didn't object when he grasped my leg under the knee and lifted it. He sunk even deeper, and I felt a brief flare of pain that quickly disappeared. His strokes were turning faster and harder. I wanted to try and match his rhythm, but it was too erratic, and he was beginning to thrust so hard that I was bouncing a little on the bed.

I watched his face, fascinated by the way his head was beginning to twist and turn, the way he was starting to pant and moan. My body was doing this to him. My body was making him lose control, and I couldn't stop the smug sense of pleasure I got from it.

"Fuck," he muttered. "Oh fuck, I'm gonna come."

I lifted my head and licked his neck, and he groaned loudly and thrust hard and fast before his entire body stiffened. He threw his head back and cried my name as I felt new wetness flood my pussy. He shook and pushed in and out for another few strokes before collapsing against me. He buried his face in my neck, and I hugged him tight. He kissed my skin before rolling off of me. I laid on my back and stared up at the ceiling.

I was no longer a virgin. I reached between my legs and touched my pussy, feeling Ren's cum dripping out of me as a small smile crossed my face.

Ren leaned over me. "You okay, sweetheart?"

I nodded, and he gave me an oddly anxious look. "You sure?"

"Yes. It didn't hurt."

"Good." He kissed me and pulled me closer, nuzzling my

neck as his hand stroked from my breasts to my pussy. "Tired?"

"Yeah. I haven't slept well since Friday night. Are you leaving now?"

"Do you want me to?"

"No."

"Good." He cupped my breast, and we lay in silence for a while before he said, "Are you asleep yet?"

I laughed. "No. I'm tired, but I'm also a little, I don't know…"

He studied me. "Do you regret fucking me?"

"God, no. It was amazing. Really. Do you – was it okay for you?"

"Sweetheart, it was better than okay. It was incredible and well worth the wait. Your little pussy is so tight, I barely lasted five minutes."

"I didn't mind," I said. "Of course, I guess I don't have anything to compare it to, so…"

"Well," he leaned down and sucked at my nipple until it was hard and fresh need was blooming in my belly, "I guess we need to remedy that."

His hand slipped between my legs and rubbed at my clit, and I moaned and clutched at his arm. "You want me again?"

"Sweetheart, I never stop wanting you."

I studied his face before pressing a kiss against his mouth. "Mads was right. You are sweet. The sweetest man I've ever met."

He grinned at me. "Let me show you how sweet I can be, Rachel."

"Yes, Ren."

"Rachel, wake up."

I grumbled and tried to pull the covers over my head when Ren shook my shoulder. "Go away."

He laughed. "Not a morning person. Good to know. Get up, sweetheart."

"Why?"

"Because it's eight-thirty, and you'll be late for work."

I yawned and stretched before cuddling up against Ren. "I don't work until noon today."

"Shit. I woke you up for nothing."

"That's okay. I can think of something to do until I go to work." I reached under the covers and stroked Ren's dick. He hardened immediately, and I pouted at him when he pulled my hand away.

"What's wrong? Do you have to go to work?"

He shook his head. "No, not until later this afternoon."

"Then we have plenty of time for sex." I didn't understand his hesitancy. We'd had sex three times last night, and from what I'd heard from Madison, guys loved morning sex.

"No, sweetheart."

My heart dropped into my stomach. Shit, was he tired of me already?

He must have seen the sick look on my face because he cupped my face and pressed a kiss against my mouth. "Only because you're too sore. Not because I don't want you."

"I'm not sore," I protested as Ren climbed out of the bed and walked naked toward my attached bathroom. "Ren, I'm not sore."

"You will be as soon as you start moving around," he said. "I'm going to run you a bath. Stay in bed."

I relaxed in bed, both a little miffed that he wouldn't fuck me again and happy that he was being so sweet to me. He returned in less than fifteen minutes and pulled the covers back. "C'mon, sweetheart. Climb into the bath while I make us some breakfast."

I slid out of bed and started toward the bathroom. I winced and stumbled, and Ren slipped his arm around my waist. Shit. He was right. I was sore. At least my thigh muscles were, anyway. My pussy felt a little sore, but it was my legs that were yelling in outrage. God, I needed to work out more.

"You okay?"

"Fine," I said grumpily. "I'm not sore."

He laughed. "Then why are you limping?"

"I have some mild discomfort in my thighs, and I believe I mentioned to you last night that I was a wimp."

He laughed again, and I grinned at him when he kissed the tip of my nose. "I added some Epsom salts to your bath. Climb in, little wimp, and soak away your aches and pains."

"Are you sure you got enough to eat?"

I grinned at Ren before opening the dishwasher and loading my empty bowl. "Plenty. The oatmeal, pancakes, fruit and toast are about ten times what I normally eat for breakfast."

"Breakfast is the most important meal of the day." He cleared the table, handing me each dish to put in the dishwasher before rinsing the dishcloth and wiping down the table.

"You made breakfast. I should be doing the clean-up," I protested.

"I don't mind." He joined me at the counter, rinsing the cloth again and hanging it neatly over the sink.

He had gotten dressed before breakfast, but I had thrown

on my nightgown after my bath. I'd deliberately not worn a bra or panties in the hopes of convincing Ren to fuck me one more time. My thighs were still a little sore, but I didn't care. Just being around Ren made me horny, and I wanted more of what only he could give me.

"I should probably get going. You have to be at work in an hour and a half." Ren was studying me, and I wondered if I imagined his ask-me-to-stay look.

I decided there was only one way to find out.

I stepped closer, relieved when Ren automatically put his arms around my waist. I nuzzled his neck. "I have a better idea. Why don't you come to the bedroom, and I'll say thank you for running me a bath and making me breakfast."

One big hand slid under my nightgown and squeezed my bare ass. "I don't want to make you late for work."

"You won't." I licked his throat, enjoying the way his breath hissed out and the feel of his hardening dick against my stomach. "Don't you want to know how I'll say thank you?"

He grinned at me before dipping his head and kissing me. I moaned when his tongue invaded my mouth and sucked at it as he rubbed me against his erection.

"Does it involve your hot little mouth?" he whispered against my lips.

"It might." I licked his bottom lip and then sucked on it. God, Ren was turning me into a sex addict. "If, you know, you want me to, um, please you orally?

Oh.My.God.

Ren's laugh sent both lust and embarrassment through me.

"Oh shit. That was the least sexiest way to offer a blow job ever, wasn't it?"

"Sweetheart, almost everything you say turns me on, but we could work on your dirty talk."

"I'm sorry. I'm horrible at this."

"You're not." He bent his head and kissed a trail down my throat before licking along my collarbone. "You just need practice. Repeat after me."

I squeaked when his other hand cupped my breast through my nightgown, and his fingers played with my nipple. I could feel my pussy getting wet as I let my head fall back so Ren could kiss my throat again. He was talking, but I couldn't hear past the rapid pounding of my heartbeat.

He pinched my nipple, and I squealed loudly.

"Pay attention, sweetheart."

"I'm trying. Stop playing with my nipple so I can concentrate."

He laughed and tugged on my nipple again. "Focus, sweetheart and repeat after me." He bent his head, and his voice was muffled against my throat. In between soft nips and licks, he said, "I want your cock in my mouth, Ren."

I turned bright red but whispered, "I want your cock in my mouth, Ren."

"Louder."

I cleared my throat and tried again. "I want your cock in my mouth, Ren."

He cupped and kneaded my breast until I was moaning and arching my back. He pushed one thigh between my legs, and I shamelessly rubbed my bare pussy against him. "Good girl. Try this one… Please let me suck your extra-large cock, Ren."

I dissolved into giggles and poked him in the back. "Seriously?"

He winked at me before kissing me. "Fine. Please let me suck your cock, Ren."

"Please let me suck your cock, Ren."

"I need you to be louder, sweetheart." He tried for a disapproving tone but didn't stop me from humping his thigh. He kissed my neck and exposed upper chest again as he teased my nipple through the soft cotton of my nightgown.

Fuck. The feel of his hands, the rough fabric of his jeans against my clit had me suddenly, achingly close to an orgasm.

"Ren," I gasped. "Ren, I…"

"Say it, sweetheart." One big hand pressed against my lower back, holding me still. I whined my disappointment, and he nipped my throat. "Say it, and then I'll let you rub your little pussy on my leg until you come. That's what you really want, isn't it? You want to come all over my thigh? Mark me with your sweet cream?"

"Yes," I moaned. "Yes, I want that."

"Then tell me what I want to hear."

"Please let me suck your cock, Ren."

The relentless pressure of his hand on my back didn't let up. Feeling delirious with need – I had been so fucking close – I almost shouted it the second time. "Please let me suck your cock, Ren. Please! Please let me -"

"Rachel!"

I screamed, my body jerking against Ren's. He pushed me behind him as he swung around to face the person who had shouted my name. His body stiffened, and he muttered, "fuck" under his breath.

I peered around him, my jaw dropping open. "Mom? What the fuck are you doing here?"

Her eyebrows almost disappeared into her hairline. "You watch your filthy mouth, young lady."

"I've told you a million times that you can't just walk into my house unannounced." My embarrassment and – I'll admit it – anger at being interrupted made my usual tone with my mother harsh and resentful.

"Of course I can. I'm your mother. What are you doing with him?" She studied Ren, and when her gaze fell on the bulge at his crotch and the wet spot on the thigh of his jeans, her mouth drew down in repulsion. "Tell me you did not let him have his disgusting way with you, Rachel Eugene Banks."

Her casual dismissal of my rule and how she spoke about and looked at Ren fired my anger into something uncontrollable.

Unstoppable.

"Get out," I snarled. "Get out of my house right now."

Ren's hand took mine, and I gripped it tightly, grateful for his silent support. "Give me your key and leave. Immediately."

My mother's mouth dropped open. "No. Not until you hear what I have to say."

"I'm done listening to you. I'm done letting you tell me what to do, what to say, or how to act. This is my life, and who I sleep with – no, who I *fuck* is none of your business. I don't care what you say or how you feel about Ren. I love him, and I -"

"He's a convict!"

I stared wide-eyed at my mother. "What?"

"He's a convict, Rachel. That's why I'm here – to warn you. He's been in prison, and I am not allowing my only child to be with someone like him. He's not good enough for you."

Ren dropped my hand, and I turned to him. The look of shame on his face made me want to cry, but when I tried to touch him, he twisted away.

"Ren? Is it true?"

"Of course it's true," my mother snapped.

I ignored her and took another step toward Ren. He

backed away, and my heart twisted in my chest. "Ren, say something.'

"It's true." The words fell from his mouth like bricks. "It's true, Rachel."

I stared dumbfoundedly at him, and he grabbed his jacket from the chair. He walked toward the door, ignoring my mother when she skittered out of the doorway and into the kitchen and gave him a look of fear.

"Ren!"

He paused in the doorway and gave me another brief, shame-filled glance that broke my heart. "I'm sorry."

He left the kitchen, and a few seconds later, the front door slammed. I slumped against the counter, staring blankly at the floor. Ren had been in prison. The quiet, sweet man I was in love with had been in prison.

I guess I should have felt disgust, maybe. Or was it anger or hurt I was supposed to be feeling? Ren had lied to me about –

No, he didn't lie. You never specifically asked him if he'd been in prison. You've barely asked him anything. You were too busy using him for your own needs, weren't you? You're in love with him, but you can't even take the time to have one damn conversation with him? You're just panting after him like a bitch in heat.

I winced, but my inner voice wasn't wrong about any of it.

Still, shouldn't I have been angry with him for keeping something like that from me?

Maybe. But instead, all I felt was sorrow and an ache in the pit of my stomach. The way Ren had looked, ashamed and sad and guilty, made me feel awful. It ate a hole into my stomach, and I wanted to comfort him, to assure him that it didn't matter to me what his past was.

I took a deep breath as the truth of it hit me. It didn't

matter. I didn't care what Ren had done or why he'd been in prison. I would ask him, and if he wanted to tell me then fine. If he didn't, I wouldn't push him about it. All that mattered to me was who he was now. A good, sweet man who didn't love me the way I loved him but made me feel loved anyway.

"I can't believe you thought your mother would lie to you. You've always been too naïve and trusting. You think I smother you, but you need me, Rachel."

I blinked at my mother. I had almost forgotten she was there, even though she hadn't shut up since Ren left.

"I just knew if I left you to your own devices, you would screw this up. I can't believe you were having relations with that *man*. Do you have any idea what you've done, Rachel? When word gets out that you slept with him, a bartender and a convict, my reputation will be destroyed in this town."

"His name is Ren, and I love him."

My mother gaped at me. "Stop it. Stop being so difficult. Now, go wash his filth off, and then you and I will see Father McRoy. You'll confess all of your disgusting -"

"I'm not going anywhere with you, let alone to the church we haven't set foot in since Dad left fifteen years ago."

My mother paled. "Don't you talk about him."

"He left, Mom. He left both of us, and it's time for you to get over it and stop interfering in my life. I know you're lonely and angry, but you need to figure out how to fix your-self and stop trying to fix me."

I walked toward her and cupped her arms, squeezing gently. "It's not your fault that Dad left, okay? Stop beating yourself up about it and -"

My mother yanked away from me and gave me a disdainful look. "Of course, it's not my fault. It's yours. You were a terrible baby and an awful child, and all of my attention went to you. Your father cheated on me because I was too busy with you. If you'd been a good baby, a well-behaved child, then your father would never have left me. I would have had more time to see to his needs. I've been alone for fifteen years because of you, Rachel."

I was struck silent for the second time in less than fifteen minutes. I knew my mother had never gotten over my father leaving us, but I had no idea she blamed me. She was right – I was a naïve little fool.

"You hate me." My voice was dull and heavy. "All these years, you've actually hated me."

"Don't be ridiculous. I've never hated you."

"But you don't love me." I stared up at her, my stomach churning when I saw the answer in her eyes.

She looked away. "Get dressed. We're going to church, and you're -"

"Stop, Mom." My voice was gentle and low. "Just stop."

She studied me for a moment, and I shook my head when she opened her mouth. "We're done."

"What do you mean?"

"I love you, but I can't do this anymore. I need you to leave and not contact me again."

"You don't mean that."

"I do."

Her gaze narrowed. "You ungrateful little bitch. All that I've done for you and given up for you, and you're telling me I don't have the right to see you."

I nodded. "Yes. For now. Maybe in a few months -"

"*Months?*"

"Maybe in a few months, we'll talk again. But right now, we both need space. Don't call me, don't text me, don't come and see me. I won't let you into the house."

"You're abandoning your mother for a man? A worthless -"

"Don't. Don't call Ren worthless." My voice was harsh, and my mother chewed at her bottom lip before giving me a smoking look of hatred.

"You're no better than your father. I guess the apple doesn't fall far from the tree, does it? You're leaving me just like he did for nothing more than a bit of dirty, filthy sex."

I didn't say anything. I couldn't say anything. The venom and anger spewing from my mother had rendered me silent, and I just wanted her to leave.

I wanted to be free.

"He's a convict, Rachel! You can't possibly want to be with someone like that."

"How did you find out?" I asked. "Did you hire someone to dig into his past, or did you do the dirty work yourself?"

"All you have to do is Google his name, Rachel! He's a bad person and -"

"He's not. He's a good man, and I love him. I won't apologize for that."

"He doesn't love you. You're not pretty enough for a man like him. He's used to thin girls with pretty faces."

For the first time in my life, her jabs about my looks didn't bother me. I may not have been thin or had a pretty face, but Ren wanted me. He wanted me, and he thought I was beautiful. There was no doubt in my mind about that.

"Fine," my mother suddenly spat. "I'll do what you're asking, but I hope you're prepared to come crawling back to me on your knees when that awful bartender breaks your heart. When he tells you that you're fat and ugly and stupid. When he -"

"He won't say that to me," I said. "You're the only one who tells me I'm fat and ugly and stupid."

Her face flushed, and she straightened her shoulders before marching toward the kitchen door.

"Mom?"

She turned, her face already triumphant and smug.

"The key. Give it back."

She hesitated, and I sighed. "I'll just change the locks."

She dug in her purse and pulled out the key, throwing it on the floor in a fit of temper. "You're going to regret this decision."

"Goodbye, Mom."

CHAPTER 7

Ren

"**Y**ou need to slow down."

I glared at Jack and deliberately tipped the shot of whiskey down my throat. It burned its way down my esophagus before joining the first two shots in my stomach.

He rolled his eyes and put his feet on my worn coffee table before drinking some beer. "Don't give me that look. Tell me what's wrong."

"Nothing."

"Bullshit. You're supposed to be at work, but you're home, sitting in the dark and getting drunk."

"I just wanted a night off. What's the big deal?"

"You never just take a night off. Stop being a dick and tell me what the fuck is wrong."

"How did you know I was home and not at work?"

"Jesus, the whiskey is making you stupid." Jack took

another drink of beer. "Lily and I stopped in at the bar for a drink. You weren't there. I got worried."

"Now, who's the bullshitter?" I stared at the whiskey bottle, contemplating whether I should pour myself another shot.

"Fine. That waitress, the one who's fucking Jacob Marken, what's her name again?"

"Madison."

"Right. She told me you and Rachel had a fight, and you didn't come in to work."

"I'm firing her for telling you that."

Jack laughed. "Yeah, right. You're so fucking soft-hearted, it makes me cringe. How the fuck we're even friends, I'll never know."

"You *are* an asshole."

"Don't I know it." Jack raised his beer to me. "But I'm the asshole who's always had your back, so tell me what the fuck you fought with Rachel about. And Jesus, have you even fucked her yet? Tell me you have, or I'm taking away your goddamn man card."

"We were together last night," I admitted.

"So, what? Your little pecker wasn't enough for her, and she got pissed?" He gave me a good-spirited grin. "Don't feel bad. Not everyone can have a monster dick like 'ole Jack."

He grabbed his crotch, and despite how miserable I was, I couldn't help but grin. "You're *such* an asshole."

"Yep."

I stared at the bottle of whiskey again. "It was good. Really good, you know? She might have been a virgin, but she was so…she was incredible."

Fuck, I sounded like an idiot, but I didn't know how else to explain it. After the third round of sex, Rachel had fallen sound asleep, but I had stayed awake like a love-struck fool and just stared at her. I was falling for her and falling goddam hard, and I had no idea how to stop it.

I didn't want to stop it.

I wanted Rachel. I loved Rachel.

I cleared my throat. "Anyway, it was perfect, and the next morning, I ran her a bath and cooked her breakfast and -"

Jack laughed and held out his beer bottle to me again. "Pussy-whipped already."

I glared at him, but he gave me another good-natured grin. "Hey, welcome to the club. The other day, I fucking went clothes shopping with Lily. Held her goddamn purse and everything."

I laughed, and Jack shrugged. "It feels good to do something for the woman you love. Doesn't it?"

I nodded. "I love her, Jack. I do."

"Yeah, that's been fucking obvious for the last three years. So, what happened?"

"Her mother stopped by and told her I'd been in prison."

"Shit. How the fuck did she find out?"

I shrugged. "I'm sure it wasn't difficult. There were articles in the newspaper and online about it. The cops had been trying to bust Tony for a long time, so it was a big deal when they did."

"You were pretty low down on the chain," Jack said. "For fuck's sake, you only did four years."

"Yeah, but I'm sure my name was mentioned in at least one article." I reached for the bottle of whiskey and poured a shot. I stared at the amber liquid. "Anyway, Rachel's mother found out I was an ex-convict, and she told Rachel."

"What did Rachel say?"

"She wanted to know if it was true, and I said yes."

"Then what?"

"I left."

"What?"

"I left." I studied Jack over the shot of whiskey.

"Why?"

"What do you mean, why? You think Rachel's going to want to be with me after this? The look on her face…"

"What about it?"

"She was shocked and upset."

"Angry?"

I just shrugged. Truthfully, I had no idea if she'd been angry or not. My own anger at Rachel's mother, my shame at Rachel finding out what a fuck-up I was, had made my memory of Rachel's reaction a little fuzzy.

Or maybe that was the whiskey.

The doorbell rang as I lifted the shot to my lips. Jack glanced at my front door. "Expecting someone?"

I shook my head. "Ignore it."

"You don't need that shot," Jack said as he stood up.

Maybe I didn't need it, but I sure as fuck wanted it. "Don't answer it," I said when the doorbell rang again.

Jack flipped me the bird and crossed the room to the door. I pressed the glass to my lips and then spit whiskey all over the coffee table when Jack opened the door, and I saw Rachel's sweet face. I wiped my mouth, jumping to my feet, as Jack grinned at her.

"Hey, Rachel."

"Um, hi." She gave him a nervous look. "You're, uh, Jack, right?"

"That's right."

"I was looking for Ren. Is he home?"

"He's right here. Come on in." Jack stepped back and grinned at me as Rachel stepped into my house. I immediately wanted to pick her up and carry her to my bedroom. How many times had I fantasized about this moment? About having her in my bed, her scent on my sheets?

My cock hardened, and I wiped my mouth again as Rachel gave me a small smile.

"Hi, Ren."

"Hey."

She chewed on her bottom lip before glancing at Jack. "I just stopped in to, um… that is, if you're busy…"

"He's not. I was just leaving." Jack opened the door, and he was gone before I could stop him.

"Um, hi," Rachel said. She stared at my small living room. "I like your place."

"It's not as nice as your place."

"No, it's nice. Really nice."

I just shrugged and stared at the puddle of whiskey on my coffee table. "You want something to drink?"

"No, thank you."

"Why aren't you at work?"

"I worked until six and then asked Barb if I could leave early. Why aren't you at work? Madison texted me and said you didn't come in."

"I didn't feel like going in," I said.

"May I sit down?"

I shrugged again. "If you want."

I expected her to sit in the armchair. When she joined me on the small couch, sitting right next to me, the heat of her thigh against mine made me panic. I tried to move away, and she put one hand on my thigh.

I groaned. I couldn't help it. Just being near her had me so fucking horny I couldn't think straight.

"Ren, look at me."

I didn't want to, but I forced my gaze to hers. There was

heat in it, and my balls tightened when Rachel's hand rose higher on my thigh. "Do you know why I'm here?"

I shook my head. I was mesmerized by the curve of her lower lip and the tip of her tongue as it darted out to wet the upper one.

"I'm here because I never did get to thank you for making me breakfast this morning. I'm here to suck your cock."

"What?" My voice was full of hoarse disbelief. "What did you say?"

She smiled, showing her even white teeth before wetting her lower lip this time. "Please let me suck your cock, Ren."

Her soft hand covered my crotch, and I hissed out a breath when she rubbed my erection. She leaned in to kiss me, and I pulled away, grabbing her hand and yanking it off my dick. "Stop."

"You don't want me anymore?"

I hated the hurt I could hear in her voice. "No. God, no, that's not it."

"Then what's the problem?"

I stared at her in disbelief. What the hell was happening?

"Let me suck your cock, Ren," she repeated. My cock surged against my jeans, and I winced at the pressure.

"What are you doing, Rachel?"

"I think I've made it clear."

"We can't."

"Why not?"

"Because!"

"Because, why?"

Her voice was relentless. Just like her hand sliding up toward my cock.

"Rachel, please."

Something in my voice must have upset her because she pulled her hand away and crossed her arms over her torso as she blinked back tears. "I'm sorry about what happened with my mother. I took back her key so that it won't happen again. If you would give me another chance, I swear we won't keep getting interrupted by her. In fact, I'm not even talking -"

"Rach," I took her arms and gave her a gentle shake, "this has nothing to do with your mother interrupting us and everything to do with the fact that I'm an ex-convict."

"Oh, thank God," she said.

I blinked at her. "Thank God?"

"I thought you were rejecting me because we keep getting interrupted by my mother, like I'm a stupid teenage girl, not because of the convict thing."

"The convict thing? Rachel, I was in prison. Do you understand that?"

"Yes." She gave me a miffed look. "I'm not an idiot, Ren."

"You shouldn't be here."

"Why? Because you're an ex-convict?"

"Yes!"

She rolled her eyes. "I don't care about your past."

"What?"

I knew my mouth had dropped open, and I shut it with a snap when Rachel giggled and said, "Close your mouth, Ren, you're gonna catch flies."

She took my hand and squeezed it. "That's something my Dad used to say. Honestly, I don't remember him very well anymore. I was eight when he left, but my mother burned all his pictures, and my memories of him have grown increasingly fuzzy. It makes me feel bad, you know? That I can't even remember his face. Sometimes I remember the sound of his voice, but even that's fading."

She gave me a sad smile. "I don't care what my mother says. It isn't my fault."

"What isn't your fault?"

"It doesn't matter. Just like your past doesn't matter."

She took my hands and tugged on them. "Come on. Take me to your bedroom."

"Rach, no, I can't."

"Can't or won't?"

"I'm not good enough for you."

"Bullshit." She squeezed my hands again. "You're the best thing that's ever happened to me, Ren Parker, and I'm not letting you go this easy. I don't care that you've been in prison. Do you care that I stole a mascara tube from Walgreens when I was fifteen?"

"It's not the same."

She just shrugged, and now it was my turn to squeeze her hands. "Don't you even want to know what I did, or did your mother tell you?"

"She didn't tell me. She tried to, and I wouldn't let her."

"Why?"

"Because it isn't any of my business."

I studied her for a moment. "I want you to know."

"Then tell me," she said simply.

I tried to pull my hands away, but she shook her head. "No. Don't pull away already. Just tell me, honey."

I took a deep breath and stared at her sweet face. "My aunt and uncle raised me. My mother was a single mom, and she got into drugs and died of an overdose when I was ten. Her sister took me in, but her husband was a drunk. He beat my aunt, my cousin, and me whenever he got drunk, which was often."

"Oh, honey." She leaned forward and hugged me before I could stop her.

I wrapped my arms around her and buried my face in her throat as she stroked my back. After a few minutes, we broke apart, but when she leaned against me, I didn't stop her. I touched the thick plait of her braided hair as she wrapped her arm around my waist and rested her cheek against my chest.

"I ran away when I was sixteen. Three weeks later, my uncle was drunk and downstairs in the basement. My aunt and my cousin were upstairs in bed. My uncle passed out while smoking, and the house caught on fire. They all died."

"I'm so sorry," she said again.

I kissed the top of her head. "I lived on the streets until I got arrested for grand theft auto at nineteen."

She lifted her head and stared at me. Feeling sick to my stomach, I said, "I was working for this guy named Tony, jacking cars and bringing them back to his shop. I knew it was wrong, but I needed the money, and a part of me didn't care. I was... angry and bitter at the world."

"I'm not surprised," she said before squeezing me. "You didn't have a good life, Ren."

"Anyway, Tony ran the biggest carjacking ring in the city and the cops had been after him for a while. Eventually, his time ran out, and he and a bunch of his employees, myself included, were arrested. Because I was only nineteen, the judge was lenient. I got four to seven years with the chance of parole."

She petted my chest through my shirt. "How horrible was it in prison?"

"It wasn't great, but I got my GED while in there and stayed out of trouble. After four years, I was granted parole. My parole officer was a pretty good guy, and he helped me out a lot. He found me a place to stay and was okay with it when I got a job as a bouncer at a bar. A lot of parole officers don't like that shit. They want you to get a job in an office or at a fucking car dealership or something.

The bar owner liked me, and after about three months, he stuck me behind the bar and taught me how to be a bartender."

"Do you like being a bartender?" she asked.

"I do. I like owning my bar. After a year, I wanted a fresh start, wanted to get out of the city, you know? So, I talked to my parole officer and got his permission to move. I moved here and worked construction for a few years before Jack helped me get the loan to open my bar."

"Are you still on parole?"

I shook my head. "No, it's done. Rach, I never did anything violent. I swear. I got in a few fights here and there, but I -"

She sat up and cupped my face. "You're a good man, Ren Parker. That's more than obvious. I'm not afraid of you, and I know you're not violent. You're the sweetest man I know."

"What about your mother?"

"I'm not talking to her anymore."

"I can't be the person who comes between you and your mom. I won't -"

"You're not. I don't want to go into detail right now, but I promise to give you the whole sordid story soon," she said. "My mom is...well, let's just say I'm cutting her out of my life for me, not you."

"Are you sure?"

"God, yes." She gave me a mock look of annoyance. "It's not all about you, Ren Parker. I have my own baggage, you know."

I smiled a little before sobering. "I'm not good enough for you."

Her forehead wrinkled, and her hands squeezed my face. "Say that again to me, and I swear I'll make you eat my pussy a thousand times before I suck your dick once."

I laughed, I couldn't help it, and she beamed at me before standing up. "C'mon, handsome. Let's go to your bedroom."

"Rachel, we should talk some more."

"No, we've done enough talking for now. Come to your bedroom and let me suck your dick, Ren."

I hesitated a moment longer, and she tugged on my hands. "Do I need to get on my knees and beg?"

A slow grin crossed my face. "If you're on your knees in front of me, sweetheart, your mouth will be too full to beg."

"There you are." She gave me a cat-like look of satisfaction as I stood and took her hand.

"You are so fucking hot, sweetheart. Do you have any idea how beautiful you are?"

I smoothed Rachel's hair back as she stared up at me. After we had undressed, I had unbraided her hair, and I gathered her long tresses in one hand as I stared down at her. Fuck. Rachel, naked and on her knees with my cock in her mouth, was the most beautiful goddamn thing I'd ever seen.

"Good, sweetheart. Suck a little harder."

She sucked harder, staring up at me as I tugged lightly on her hair to guide her back and forth over my dick. She had admitted to me that she'd never had a cock in her mouth when we got to the bedroom, but goddamn, her enthusiasm for sucking my dick was overshadowing any of her awkward, not-quite-certain-what-to-do moves.

"That's good, sweetheart. Do you like sucking on my cock?"

She nodded, and I made a harsh groan, my hips thrusting forward when she hummed, and her lips vibrated around my aching dick. I pulled back, and she grinned up at me as I wiped away a mixture of my cum and her saliva from her chin.

"I read about doing that in a book. Did it feel good?"

"So good." I hauled her up into a standing position, and she pouted at me.

"Why are you making me stop?"

"I need to fuck you right now."

"Okay." She gave me a thumbs-up and hopped onto the bed.

I laughed and stretched out next to her as she studied my dick. "Can I try being on top?"

I nodded, and she straddled me a bit clumsily. I groaned when she rubbed her soaking wet pussy against my dick.

She made an unladylike grunt that did nothing to lessen my hard-on for her as she tried to push her pussy onto my dick. "Ren, help me. I can't get it in."

I winked at her before patting one smooth thigh. "Lift a bit."

She braced her hands on my chest and lifted her lower body. I grabbed my cock and rubbed the head of it against her clit.

"Oh! Oh my gosh. Maybe you should keep doing that," she moaned.

I ignored her and guided my dick to her wet, hot hole. As I pushed the head in, she made a happy little squeal and sank down, taking all of my cock in one hot push.

"Oh!"

"You okay?" I gave her a worried look, and she nodded.

"Yes, you're just really thick. I need a minute."

I tucked my hands under my head and smiled up at her. "Take all the time you need, sweetheart."

She traced her fingers over my chest, and my hips bucked when she pinched my nipple.

"Ooh, that's nice," she said.

She braced her hands against my chest again before moving up and down in a slow rhythm. I began to thrust up in time with her movements, and she moaned happily before cupping her breasts and pinching her nipples.

"Fuck!" My hands came out from under my head in a hurry, and I gripped her hips before fucking her hard and rough.

She squealed and rode my rough movements, squeezing her thighs around my waist like I was a bucking bronco.

"Touch yourself," I demanded.

She wet her lips before reaching down and rubbing her clit a bit hesitantly.

"Don't be shy, sweetheart," I said. "Touch it like you want it."

She giggled but began to rub her clit in a hard circular motion.

"Good," I said. I watched Rachel rub her clit as I fucked her, and when after only a few minutes, she began to moan and toss her head back and forth, I didn't stop her from coming. Watching Rachel come all over my cock was something I would never tire of. Her moans grew louder, and she shouted my name as her climax rushed through her. Her body stiffened, her pussy tightened exquisitely around my cock and then milked it with hard, rhythmic pulses as she came.

I cursed and thrust in and out, Rachel's squeezing wet pussy drawing my orgasm from me in a hard, roaring rush that took my breath away and made my entire body shake. I arched into her again and again until I collapsed on the bed, panting harshly.

Rachel rested her head on my chest, and I petted her hair as she rubbed my arm. After a few moments, she eased off of me. I immediately missed her soft warmth and pulled her close as she snuggled against my side.

"So good," she whispered.

"Hmm."

"It's good for you, right?" She stared up at me, and I kissed her forehead.

"Sweetheart, you have no idea. I can't get enough of you."

"Good." She rested against me again.

After a while, I shifted beneath her, and she raised her head. She studied my face and touched my jaw. "What's wrong?"

"Why do you want to be with me?"

"Because I love you."

I sucked in a hard breath. Rachel had said she loved me in her kitchen, but I didn't know if she had meant it or was saying it to piss her mother off.

"Why do you look so surprised?" she asked. "I know you heard me say it earlier."

"I didn't know if you meant it."

"Of course I meant it. I wouldn't say it if I didn't. I know you're not there yet, and I'm not trying to freak you out, I promise. I just wanted you to know that I love you."

"I love you too."

She sat up and stared at me. "Did you just say you loved me?"

"Yes."

"For real?"

"Yes."

"Like, you're in love with me, want to be with me, will let me fuck you whenever I want to, love?"

"Yes, yes, and…yes."

She laughed. "I knew it."

"You did not."

"Did, too. You're an open book when it comes to your feelings, and I, sir, am a librarian. I read books for a living."

I burst into laughter before pulling her down on top of me and kissing her hard on the mouth. "God, I love you."

"I love you too, Ren Parker."

KEEP READING FOR AN EXCERPT OF "THE WELDER," BOOK Four in the Working Men Series.

THE WELDER EXCERPT

WORKING MEN SERIES BOOK FOUR

Copyright © 2018 Ramona Gray

Luna

Now's your chance, girl. You have to tell him.

I wanted to ignore my inner voice as the big man approached the counter. It was strange to see him in the coffee shop at this time. He always stopped by in the morning, and when I didn't see him this morning, I resigned myself to the fact that I wouldn't see him today.

But now, just five minutes before my shift ended, he was walking through the doors. He was wearing his usual t-shirt and jeans, and I admired the broadness of his chest before peeking quickly at his crotch. Not sure why I looked, but damn if I didn't every time. Apparently, I was expecting, or maybe hoping, that he would just once have a noticeable woody.

Yeah, because he just can't control his reaction to you.

I sighed. Pretending that Asher Stokes was attracted to me was the stupidest thing ever, but damned if I hadn't been

249

pretending since high school. He'd never shown a single lick of interest in me, though, which made what I was about to tell him a thousand times harder.

You did it to yourself. This is what you get for lying.

My inner voice wasn't wrong, but, man, did it have to sound so judgmental?

Of course, I didn't have to tell Asher anything. I could just admit the truth to my sister when she came to town in minus three days and counting.

I could look her in the eye and say, "Lydia, I've been lying to you for the last eight months. I am not, in fact, dating Asher Stokes."

It sounded simple enough in my head, but my entire body cringed at the thought. The look she would give me, the smug smile, the "Oh, Luna, I knew it all along. If Asher didn't want me, he'd *never* want you."

She probably wasn't wrong, but that didn't mean I wanted to hear it. I had spent my entire life living in my sister's shadow, and it had felt so good to finally have something she'd always wanted but never had.

The fact that it was one giant whopper of a lie three days and four hours away from unravelling around me was a minor detail. Right?

The giant was standing before me now, and my body started shaking like it always did when he was close. Not from fear. Oh no. Even though he could have crushed me easily with one ham-sized hand, I'd never felt any fear around him.

Bone-rattling, vein-throbbing, body-shaking, lust?

Yeah, that I was familiar with.

"Hi, Asher. Your usual?" My voice was high-pitched. I fucking sounded like Minnie Mouse. Great.

"Hey. Yeah, the usual."

"Coming right up!"

His brows drew down, and he studied me thoughtfully as he pulled a few bills from his wallet.

Oh fuck. I was screwing this up royally.

Then don't talk to him. Just admit to your sister what you did and be done with it.

"No!"

"I'm sorry?" Asher gave me another confused look as he held out the bills.

Oh God, I'd said it out loud. I smoothed my shaking hands over my apron, wishing I hadn't spilled that Frappuccino all over it after lunch.

"Um, nothing," I said. I took his money and rang it through before handing him back his change. My fingers brushed against his rough palm, and my shaking increased tenfold. God, I needed to get control of my own damn body.

I turned away and poured his coffee, venti dark roast, and brought it to the other end of the counter where the man of my fucking dreams was waiting. I'd left more room than usual but had no choice with how my body was vibrating. As it was, I still spilled a bit of the hot liquid on his hand when I set the coffee down.

He made a soft hiss, and I dabbed at his hand with my fingertips, trying to, I dunno, soak up the hot liquid with my flesh because that made perfect sense.

"Oh God, I'm so sorry. Are you okay?"

"Fine."

I grabbed his hand and studied the top of it. "Do you need a bandage? We have a first-aid kit in the back with stuff for burns."

He yanked his hand away. "It's fine. I get burned all the time."

I blinked at him. "Oh, uh, right. Sorry."

Fuck, I was an idiot. The man was a welder, and his hands showed it. They were marked with small scars from burns that would have hurt a lot worse than some hot coffee.

"Bye." He picked up his coffee and turned away.

Shit, he was leaving. I had to do something, say something – "Asher?"

He turned around and studied me silently.

"Um, do you have a few minutes to talk? I'm off, uh, now, actually, and I wanted to discuss something with you."

I waited for him to say no, waited for him to decide for me whether I was humiliated in front of my sister or humiliated in front of the man I'd wanted for most of my life.

"Okay."

"I'm sorry?" I blinked up at him, certain I had misheard him. Okay sounded like no in some languages, right?

"I said okay." He repeated himself like I was slow, and honestly, I couldn't blame him.

"Oh, great. Okay, I need ten minutes. Do you mind waiting while I cash out?"

He shook his head, and I stumbled back from the counter. "Okay. Great. Okay, I'll be right back. Don't go anywhere!" I laughed like a drunk donkey having a stroke and then tripped over the box of coffee that someone – me, it was me – had left by the counter. I landed hard on my ass and popped back up immediately as my coworker Jeff rolled his eyes and kept on walking.

I resisted the urge to rub my butt as Asher stared at me. "Sorry. I'll, uh, be right back."

ABOUT THE AUTHOR

Ramona Gray is a Canadian romance author. She currently lives in Alberta with her awesome husband and her super cute dog. She's addicted to home improvement shows, good coffee, and reading and writing about the steamier moments in life.

For more information about Ramona, check out her website at

www.ramonagray.ca

facebook.com/RamonaGrayBooks
instagram.com/ramonagrayauthor
amazon.com/Ramona-Gray/e/B00OD26SAM
bookbub.com/profile/ramona-gray

ALSO BY RAMONA GRAY

The Bartender

The Welder

The Electrician

The Landscaper

The Firefighter

The Cop

The Paramedic

Sexy Scientists Series

The Chemist

The Biologist

The Physicist

The Geologist

The Paleontologist

The Botanist

Other World Series

The Vampire's Kiss (Book One)

The Vampire's Love (Book Two)

The Shifter's Mate (Book Three)

Rescued By The Wolf (Book Four)

Claiming Quinn (Book Five)

Choosing Rose (Book Six)

Elena Unbound (Book Seven)

www.ingramcontent.com/pod-product-compliance
Lightning Source LLC
Chambersburg PA
CBHW051631260626
47170CB00004B/1126